MARIA VON

MARIA VON TRAPP

and Her Musical Family

Cheri Blomquist

Illustrated by John Herreid

IGNATIUS PRESS   SAN FRANCISCO

Cover art and design by
Christopher J. Pelicano

CONTENTS

PROLOGUE

L OUD AND SHRILL, THE TRAIN WHISTLE pierced the evening air. "All aboard!" bellowed the conductor.

"It's time to go, Augusta." A graying farmer of about sixty stood up and reached a hand to the young woman next to him. "Let me help you onto the train now."

"I'm fine, Father," she replied lightly, taking hold of her carpetbag. "I can do it."

"Let him help you anyway," insisted her mother, rising and taking Augusta's other hand. "We don't want you to slip and fall, especially when the baby is coming so soon."

Together they pulled her up. Wobbling a little, Augusta held on to them a moment to steady herself and then let them guide her out the station door to the grumbling train. She shivered. It was colder than usual for late January. Her heart beat faster as anxiety suddenly gripped her. How she wished Karl had not returned to Vienna for business so soon after Christmas! As much as he needed her at home with him, she preferred to stay longer with her parents. It wouldn't do to let her parents see her feelings, though; they were worried enough already.

"I feel as if I have a big ball stuck in my stomach," she joked.

"Are you sure you are feeling well enough to travel?" fretted her mother as they made their way to the door of the sleeping car. "Couldn't we send a telegram to Karl and tell him you'll return after the baby is born?"

Augusta patted her mother's arm. "This little one isn't due for two more weeks. I will be just fine, Mother. Uncomfortable, but fine. Besides, I promised Karl I would make it home in time, so that he can be with me when the baby is born. I keep my promises!"

Her father huffed as they approached the first step into the car. "Well, I am sure Karl would understand if you decided to stay. These things aren't predictable, you know. It's a long journey to Vienna!"

Augusta turned and hugged her parents tightly. "Do not worry! Everything will be all right. Now, remember to tell Tante Sophie and Onkel Johann good-bye for me. I didn't get a chance to see them this week. Good-bye, and thank you for a lovely Christmas! I'll send a telegram just as soon as the baby is born."

Unhappily her father helped her up the steps and backed out of the car. "Well, I'm glad you have a sleeping berth, anyway," he grumbled.

"I have a whole cabin, Father," Augusta called back. "Karl is very good to me. *Auf wiedersehen!*"

With that she entered the car and made her way to her assigned cabin, her stuffed carpetbag banging against her swollen ankles. She couldn't wait to sit down again! Suddenly, she stopped. Her belly had tightened again, and she had to breathe deeply for a moment. It was worse this time, she realized. For the first time she wondered if she should have told her mother that she had been feeling strange for several hours. Maybe she was being foolish after all and should stay here until after the birth, just to be safe.

The train whistle blew again, and she heard the conductor slam the outside doors shut. In another moment the train lurched forward. Well, it's too late now, she thought, as she found her cabin. Opening the door, she sank into the narrow chair beside the window. It's only one night, she told herself, and babies liked to take their time entering the world. She had listened to women in the village talk about such things her entire life, and there was no reason to suppose her baby would be any different. All would be well. Besides, God would not abandon her. Still, a doubt niggled at Augusta's mind as she thought of the long night ahead and all the things that might go wrong.

She pushed it aside with firm resolve. Then, pulling herself to her feet, she began to arrange her belongings. The train picked up speed, and soon cottages and animals and villagers were racing past her window. She hoped there would be no delay with their arrival in Vienna. In the rugged Tyrolean mountains of Austria there could be delays of all sorts, especially in the winter.

"Good evening, *meine Dame*! Are you settling in well? I am here to collect your ticket."

Augusta looked up with a start to see the conductor standing in her doorway. She had been so focused on her increasing discomfort that she had forgotten to shut the door. Reaching for her purse on the berth, she smiled brightly and said, "Yes, of course."

His eyes widened in dismay as he noted her strained expression and awkward movements. "Oh, *meine Dame*, are you alone on the train?"

"Yes, but I am all right. The baby will wait for the hospital."

The conductor eyed her doubtfully. "My wife has brought nine children into the world, and I know how fast such plans can change. Just to be safe, I will check on you often during the night. This train is nearly empty, and I don't think a doctor or a midwife is on board. I promise to return within an hour."

"I'm sure I will be all right," Augusta reassured him with confidence, "but I do appreciate it."

It was with surprise, then, that soon after she lay down to sleep only an hour later, she could no longer deny the truth. Her baby was coming tonight! When the conductor visited her again a little while later, he took one look at her and turned on his heel to find the things he would need.

"Quickly, quickly!" he told himself, running as fast as he could through the train. This woman did not have much time, and he was all she had tonight. He shook his head in disbelief as he gathered some towels and other supplies. Never in his wildest dreams had he thought that a baby would someday be born on his train, but he hadn't helped bring nine children into the world for nothing!

On and on the train sped beneath the glittering stars.

~

It was far below freezing that high in the Alps, but the infant, swaddled in a bath towel, slept snugly in the crook of Augusta's arm. The conductor wiped his brow and smiled down at the exhausted mother.

"January 25, 1905, about 11:15 P.M.," he said. "I'll write that down for you to give the hospital. I will make sure you are taken to the first one I can find."

"No, Herr Conductor," Augusta replied firmly. "I promised my husband I would arrive on this train. He will be waiting for me at the station in Vienna, and there I will arrive!"

"But *meine Dame*," protested the weary conductor, "you need a doctor as soon as possible!"

"I can wait a few hours," Augusta assured him. "Please don't stop the train."

The conductor scratched his head and frowned. "Well, since you insist, I will honor your wishes, but I don't feel right about it."

"I appreciate that, Herr Conductor," she replied warmly. Grasping his hand, she smiled up at him. "I appreciate everything. Without you I don't know what would have happened to us. If I'd had a son, I would have named him after you."

The conductor blushed. "Oh, you are too kind. I was happy to help. I must return to my duties now, but I will return every half hour until we arrive in Vienna. I will bring some bread and hot tea for you when I come next. Congratulations, *meine Dame*!"

After he left, Augusta lay quietly, gazing at the sleeping baby. She was so beautiful, so perfect! Soon she would be hungry, thought Augusta, so she should try to sleep, too. Dutifully, she closed her eyes, but her mind was racing. She couldn't help thinking about names. Stroking the baby's downy head thoughtfully, she mulled over the names she and Karl had been considering for a girl: Lena after her mother or Maria after the Blessed Mother. Either way, Augusta would be her middle name. She tried the name aloud both ways— "Lena Augusta Kutschera" and "Maria Augusta Kutschera." Then again: "Maria Augusta Kutschera." Karl had said it sounded like a little melody when they first discussed it. She tried the name once more, liking the idea of music following her little girl wherever she went. Karl would agree, she knew.

"My little impetuous Maria," she whispered tenderly, lifting the baby's tiny hand to kiss it. "May you always walk in God's will like the Blessed Mother and trust that He will always provide—just as He did for us tonight."

I

WHEN FATHER DIDN'T COME

May 1914, nine years later

"COME, GUSTI, WE MUST HURRY HOME!" Cousin Kathy reached for Maria's hand impatiently. "Your father will arrive soon, and he will expect you to be ready."

Maria pulled her hand away and threw Kathy a pleading look. "The other girls are going to the candy store today. Couldn't I go, too, just this once?"

"No, Gusti," she replied. "I don't have time to wait for that, and neither do you. Do you want to keep your father waiting?"

Maria knew that she must answer no to such a question, but the laughing girls clustering in the school-yard were having so much fun. In another moment they would be running to Mr. Gruber's candy store two blocks away, their arms linked and coins jingling in their dress pockets. "Please, Kathy? I promise to hurry. Besides, Ingrid invited me this time! She's the nicest girl in the whole class."

"And what will you use for money, I ask you? Mine?" asked Kathy irritably. Grabbing Maria's hand again, this time with a firm grip, she turned on her heel and marched toward home. Maria lurched after her, trying to wrench her hand away. "No, I tell you," snapped Kathy again. "We have no time for that to-day!"

"We never have time," complained Maria under her breath, glancing back at the girls with regret.

"Gusti, please walk faster. I know you're disappointed, so I'll give you a piece of Tante Elisabeth's fresh *Apfelstrudel* when we get home. She made it especially in honor of your father's visit, but I don't think she'll mind. Did you have a pleasant day in school and work hard?" Kathy smiled down at her now, as if to try to make amends. Maria sighed and nodded glumly, trotting a little to keep up with her grown-up cousin. She did like *Apfelstrudel*, especially Tante Elisabeth's, but it wasn't the same as buying a bag of chocolaty *Seidenzuckerl* with the other girls.

At home Tante Elisabeth bustled about in the kitchen, clouded by steam from the stove. As the first and oldest cousin of Maria's father, as well as his closest relative, she had taken Maria into her care after his sweet wife, Augusta, had died seven years earlier. Tante Elisabeth wasn't really an aunt, of course, but Maria loved the kind woman very much. Sometimes she liked to imagine that she was her own mother, since Mother had died of pneumonia when Maria was only two years old. Setting down her school bag by the back door, Maria gave Tante Elisabeth a quick hug.

"Gusti, my darling, how was your day?" Tante Elisabeth smiled at her in welcome before shooing her out of the way.

"Good," replied Maria, deciding not to share her disappointment about the candy store. Tante Elisabeth was a loving woman but also no-nonsense. She wouldn't have much sympathy, especially not with Father coming for dinner. "What are you cooking?"

"When your father wrote to tell us he was coming, he asked me to make his favorite *Gulasch* with rolls and *Apfelstrudel*."

Suddenly, not being allowed to go to the candy store didn't seem so bad. *Gulasch* and *Apfelstrudel* on the same day? Maria couldn't wait! "Kathy said I could have a little *Apfelstrudel* when we got home. Could I please cut myself a piece and eat it in the garden?"

Tante Elisabeth motioned toward a knife on the counter. "Only a little, Gusti. I want to make sure we have enough for dessert. Then hurry into your white dress and wash your face. I don't know when Karl will arrive, and I want to make sure you're ready."

Maria grabbed a plate and the knife. Then she made a neat slice across the pastry before carefully inserting a fork beneath the piece she had cut and lifting it onto her plate. "Thank you, Tante Elisabeth!" she cried as she hurried to the back door. "I won't be long."

"Oh, and Maria?"

At the sound of her Christian name, Maria stopped and turned to face Tante Elisabeth, knowing she would be expected to listen attentively.

"Be sure to pack your overnight bag, too. Your father plans to take you to the mountains for the weekend."

The bottom seemed to drop from Maria's stomach, and her appetite vanished. "Yes, Tante Elisabeth," she replied woodenly. Slowly she made her way to the far corner of the garden as if in a daze, her dread growing with each step. In this part of the garden she had set up a pretend bakery to while away her lonely hours. Here she would make *Linzertorten*, *Sachertorten*, and other "cakes" out of mud, grass, pebbles, and sometimes even tiny wildflowers. Tante Elisabeth didn't like her to pretend, calling it "nonsense." Although Maria could play here unobserved, she didn't want to now.

As much as she looked forward to Father's visits with

all his interesting tales and his souvenirs from his many travels, she hated to be taken away from Tante Elisabeth. The places he took her were often beautiful, but they were also strange and far away. She was always homesick. When she cried for Tante Elisabeth, Father became annoyed and sometimes even angry with her, which made her even more homesick. Why could they not have a nice visit right there with Tante Elisabeth? Weren't the delicious *Gulasch* and *Apfelstrudel* enough?

Maria finished her strudel, unable to relish the apple-raisin-and-cinnamon filling and flaky pastry that she usually loved so much. But as she pondered the weekend ahead, the late May sun warmed her cheeks, and the scent of flowers and earth calmed her nerves. Finally, taking a deep breath to clear her mind, she returned to the house to prepare for Father's arrival.

Now her thoughts were whirling with possibilities. Maybe, if she could find just the right words, she could convince Father to stay at Tante Elisabeth's during his visit. What would interest him just as much as visiting scenic mountains or taking a river cruise? She pondered this question as she washed her face and brushed her long hair until it shone. Father's idea of fun was traveling around Austria. He had an apartment in Vienna that was quite a distance from Tante Elisabeth's suburb of Kagran. Even though he lived there most of the time after many years of roaming the world, he still traveled whenever he could. And he wanted Maria to enjoy going with him.

Hmm, she thought. "Maybe Father would want to stay in Vienna if I asked him to teach me games and tell me stories from his travels. Or if I ask him to take me to his apartment so that I can see his aviary again. I could even get him to teach me more of one of his favorite languages, like Swedish or Italian."

This she considered reluctantly, because Father had tried to teach her to read some Latin, and she had been so slow to learn that he had been annoyed with her.

"Gusti!" Kathy called up the stairs. "Come help Tante Elisabeth in the kitchen now. Your father will be here soon."

After putting on the little gold cross necklace her father had given her for Christmas, Maria obediently went downstairs and tied an apron over her white, low-waisted dress. She set the table and filled the glasses, and then she finished the history lesson her teacher had assigned. When Tante Elisabeth's other daughter, Anni, came home from her job as a secretary, everyone prepared to eat.

But Father did not come.

Both annoyed and concerned, Tante Elisabeth tended the *Gulasch* and kept the rolls warm in the oven until everyone's bellies growled. Finally, she said, "It is getting so late that we had better go ahead and eat without Karl. He must have had an unexpected delay. I will give him his dinner when he arrives."

Tante Elisabeth, Maria, Kathy, and Anni ate the delicious *Gulasch* and rolls, but they decided to wait for

Maria's father to arrive before enjoying their coffee and the *Apfelstrudel*. After dinner, they all worked together to clean the kitchen, and then Maria finished her homework.

Still, Father did not arrive.

After the family ate their strudel in silence, it was time for Maria to go to bed. "Perhaps," said Tante Elisabeth, "he will arrive tomorrow. Surely something important is keeping him. He will explain it to us, and it will all make sense." Her voice was light, but as she turned away, Maria saw worry in her eyes. Suddenly, Maria was worried, too. Where was Father? He lived on the other side of Vienna, but that wasn't very far. He had never been this late before.

The next morning at school was long and boring. Maria struggled to concentrate on her lessons as she wondered why Father had not come as he said he would. Did he change his mind about wanting to see her? Maybe he was tired of trying to amuse a dull little girl like her; after all, he didn't want her to live with him as other fathers and daughters did. But at last lunchtime and recess came, and she happily played snap ball with the other girls in the schoolyard. All thoughts of Father vanished as she tried to keep the ball away from the other team. Games always cheered her up.

Maria returned to her classes feeling much better. Arithmetic would be interesting today, she decided, for the class was learning about fractions. Maria had always enjoyed puzzling out fraction problems. The hour had scarcely begun when the school headmaster, Herr Bauer, stepped into the classroom and politely cleared his throat to catch Frau Schuster's attention.

"Yes, Herr Bauer?" she asked, a touch of irritation in her voice. Frau Schuster was well liked by everyone, but she couldn't abide interruptions, even from the headmaster.

"Please forgive the intrusion, Frau Schuster. May I please see Maria Kutschera in the hall?"

Maria started with surprise, and all the children turned to stare at her. The headmaster wanted to see *her*? Slowly she stood up and took a step toward Herr Bauer.

"Please bring your belongings with you, Maria," he told her and then disappeared from the room.

Confused, Maria glanced at her teacher, who watched her with concern. "Good-bye, Maria," she said. "I hope you'll return tomorrow. Don't worry about the lesson. I'll give you extra time to learn it."

"Thank you," Maria whispered, wondering if she would be back tomorrow. What was happening?

When she stepped through the door, she was surprised to find Tante Elisabeth waiting for her in the hall. In her arms she carried Maria's spring coat and hat, as well as her schoolbag. Maria's eyes traveled from her arms to her face, where she saw redness in her eyes.

"Tante Elisabeth?" she asked cautiously.

"Thank you, Herr Bauer," Tante Elisabeth said to the headmaster. "I will speak to you again soon."

Herr Bauer gave a stiff bow, his face solemn yet gentle. "Please let me know what I can do to help, Frau Maier. I am at your service." Then, with a quick, light touch on Maria's shoulder, he turned and left.

Tante Elisabeth slid her arm around Maria's shoulders and guided her to the big doors that led out of the school. Fear flowed through Maria. As kind as she was, Tante Elisabeth seldom showed physical affection. "Where are we going, Tante Elisabeth?" asked Maria, suddenly afraid of the answer. "What's happened?"

Tante Elisabeth was silent until they had left the school grounds. Maria did not dare to ask again. Finally, Tante Elisabeth cleared her throat. "I have some very bad news, Maria," she said.

"Wh-what is it?" When Tante Elisabeth was silent again, an idea began to form at the back of Maria's mind. "Is . . . is it about Father?"

"Yes, Maria."

Maria waited, dread creeping across her stomach and down her spine.

Tante Elisabeth led her into the little park across the street and sat her down on a bench. She turned to Maria and placed her hand gently on her arm. "Kathy and I received a visit from a policeman late this morning. He told us why your father did not arrive last night."

Maria was silent, her eyes riveted on the tears that now trickled down Tante Elisabeth's cheeks.

"His maid found him this morning in a chair in his parlor. He . . ." She cleared her throat again, but her voice shook anyway when she continued. "He had passed away during his nap yesterday."

Maria stared at Tante Elisabeth, uncomprehending. "Passed away?"

"Yes, Gusti," she replied gently. "That means he died. The doctor who examined him said it was heart failure. His heart just stopped beating."

Maria tried to make sense of what Tante Elisabeth was saying. "But . . . how could it just stop? He was old but not very much, not like a wrinkled man with gray hair. I don't understand."

Tante Elisabeth wrapped her in a hug. "I don't either, my precious Gusti. Perhaps he had a heart condition that his doctor never noticed. I'm so sorry."

Feeling numb, Maria laid her head against Tante Elisabeth's shoulder and closed her eyes. In the maple tree above them a bird trilled joyously. She wondered what kind it was and felt an odd compulsion to learn about birds. Then she could forget about her father and death and the wild emotions that were rising within her from somewhere deep inside. Nothing bad could happen when studying birds.

But with those wild emotions rose a question that grew louder and louder in her mind. Tears began to well in her eyes, and her throat squeezed tightly as she said, "Now I have no mother *and* no father. What's going to happen to me, Tante Elisabeth?"

Tante Elisabeth smiled reassuringly. "I don't know, my dear, but you still have a home with me for now."

Then she lightly tapped Maria's nose. "And I promise you one thing. Hear me now."

Sniffling a bit, Maria looked at her aunt hopefully.

"I promise you that no matter what happens, God will watch over you. He will always . . . *always* . . . take care of you."

2

A HEART HARDENED

October 1916

PURE GOLD WAS THE ONLY WAY to describe the brilliant fall afternoon as Maria wandered down the street toward home and weekend freedom. With the warm, melting sunshine spilling around her, she drew in a long breath. On any other day she would be happy enough in such exquisite autumn weather, but today was special because she had just been to Mr. Gruber's candy store with the other girls in her class and had bought a small sack of *Seidenzuckerl.*

Trips to the candy store and sometimes to the bakery to gaze at the cakes in the window were no longer forbidden, now that Maria was in her fifth year. Tante Elisabeth and Kathy had decided she was ready for a little freedom once or twice a week. Usually, they could not afford to give her any money for treats, but Maria was content to spend time with her friends. Besides, they always gave her a few bites of their treats, so she never felt left out. Today, though, she had her own money. She had earned it herself by hemming a skirt for Anni.

Home was in sight now, so Maria picked up her pace, invigorated by the crisp air and crunching leaves. How different life was now from a few months ago! The heartache of losing Father had faded enough for her to feel happy again most of the time, and life had gone on as before, comfortable and secure with Tante Elisabeth, Kathy, and Anni. She was grown up enough to enjoy outings with her friends and to earn a little money with her new sewing skills, and she liked Frau Lang, her pretty teacher. God was smiling down on her, it seemed. Perhaps He was even hugging her.

"Tante Elisabeth, I'm home!" she cried, bursting through the back door, expecting to see her at the stove as usual. The smell of rich beef broth filled the air from the pot simmering on the stove. "Kathy!" No one answered, so Maria popped her head into the parlor. "Tante?"

"Not here," came a gruff voice. Maria jumped. On the other side of the room, sitting straight and still in the shadows by the fireplace, Onkel Franz watched her with knitted brows.

"Oh . . . hello, Onkel Franz," she said timidly, her stomach turning cold. She had forgotten all about him in the glory of the crisp autumn afternoon. Anni had married Franz only a month ago, and they had decided to live in Tante Elisabeth's house for reasons Maria didn't understand. Onkel Franz had an important job as a judge at the courthouse in downtown Vienna, so it seemed to Maria that he would be rich enough to have his own home. Yet Anni and he had moved upstairs to the large bedroom. It would only be for a while, they said, but they didn't seem to be in any hurry to buy their own house. Maria loved sweet, gentle Anni with all her heart, but Onkel Franz was serious and stern. She couldn't help hoping that they would soon tire of living in Tante Elisabeth's house.

"Gusti, is that you?" Tante Elisabeth called from the top of the stairs. Slowly, she made her way down as Maria replied, "Yes, Tante Elisabeth. I just got home. Look what I brought for you!"

Tante Elisabeth smiled as Maria held up the little white bag of candy. "Most of it is *Seidenzuckerl*, because they're my favorite, but I remembered that you and Kathy love *Wiener Zuckerl*, so I brought you a few pieces."

"That is very generous of you, Gusti!" Tante Elisabeth said, patting Maria's cheek when she reached the bottom step. "We'll enjoy it after dinner. Did you have fun with your friends and behave yourself in Mr. Gruber's store?"

"Of course!" Maria was indignant. After all, she was nearly ten years old and knew how to behave in a candy store. "Guess what Ingrid told me? She said—"

"Never mind that now," Tante Elisabeth interrupted, hurrying away to the kitchen. "Set the table for me, will you? Supper will be ready in about ten minutes. You can tell me while we eat."

"Okay." As Maria followed her, the icy feeling in her stomach increased. Somehow she could feel Onkel Franz' eyes on her back. For a moment she felt sorry for the grown-ups who had to endure his piercing gaze during court trials. She was glad he wasn't judging her!

Tante Elisabeth's *Tafelspitz* was good, as was all her cooking. To Maria, though, the savory beef and potatoes had the consistency of dirt in her mouth. Something about Onkel Franz was different tonight; she wasn't sure what. Not that he had ever been friendly. From the day she met him, just before his wedding to cousin Anni, he had made her uneasy with his stiff posture, cold, blue eyes, and ruler-straight mouth. Calling him "Onkel" as Tante Elisabeth demanded felt like lying, and not because he wasn't her uncle; after all, Tante Elisabeth wasn't really her aunt, only her father's cousin. Unlike Tante Elisabeth, though, he wasn't warm and kind and protective. An uncle, Maria thought, even a pretend one, should at least be something like Tante Elisabeth.

As the dishes were passed around the table, Maria eyed him cautiously. He said little, but something about him seemed strange. Perhaps it was the expression on his face. His eyes held an unusual, icy light, and his mouth curved slightly upward without becoming a smile, reminding her of a cat. That wasn't all, but Maria couldn't figure out what else about him bothered her. She only knew that she wasn't hungry anymore and wanted to go upstairs to finish her homework or even to the kitchen to wash dishes—anything to get away from Onkel Franz. Tante Elisabeth, Anni, and Kathy seemed to notice nothing out of the ordinary. They spoke of Anni's day at the bank, where she spent her days as a secretary, and of Tante Elisabeth's conversation with Frau Mueller at the market that day. Her son's wife had just delivered triplets, you see, and they were having trouble finding a nanny who would—

"Starting Monday, Maria, you are to come straight home after school each and every day," interrupted Onkle Franz. "No more dallies with other children. No more candy stores and bakeries. Is that understood?"

Conversation stopped as if it had never begun, and Maria's fork froze inside her mouth. Her eyes widened as she gaped at him in shock. Slowly she put her fork on her plate. "But . . . why, Onkel Franz?"

Tante Elisabeth, Anni, and Kathy fixed Onkel Franz with baffled stares. Tante Elisabeth flicked her eyes to Maria and then back to Onkel Franz, who continued to eat his dinner as if he had not said a word. Wiping her mouth with her napkin, she cleared her throat. "Franz, Maria has always been a good girl, coming home right after school. We decided—the three of us, before you and Anni married—that Maria was old enough to enjoy an occasional little outing with—"

"But I am her guardian, am I not?" Onkel Franz fixed his steely eyes on Tante Elisabeth as if he were conjuring a spell to make her agree with him. "Is it not my right—my duty—to decide what is best for her?"

Maria looked at Tante Elisabeth in surprise. "My guardian? Tante Elisabeth, I thought you were my guardian. You and Anni and Kathy."

Onkel Franz buttered a piece of his roll and took a bite. He chewed thoughtfully, as if he hadn't heard Maria.

Kathy smiled at Maria apologetically, as Tante Elisabeth and Anni gazed down at their plates. "Your father named Onkel Franz your guardian in his will. They were good friends for years, you know—long before Anni married him—and your father decided that Onkel Franz would be the best person to handle his affairs if he should die. He will handle all your needs from now on—school, clothes, the money your father left you . . . all those kinds of things. Tante Elisabeth and I will still take care of you from day to day, but Onkel Franz has the final say in how you are raised."

"But why would Father want him to take care of me?" persisted Maria. "I never even met him before this summer."

"Maria," Tante Elisabeth said, "you are beginning to sound impertinent."

"I," said Onkel Franz slowly between bites of bread, "am your guardian because your father said so." He pointed his knife at Maria. "And you will be grateful and respectful to me. Is that understood?"

Maria gazed down at her lap, her dinner forgotten. "Yes, Onkel Franz. But . . . why can't I visit with any of my friends after school? I've waited years to be able to do this."

Tante Elisabeth gave a guilty little sigh but said nothing. Anni kept very still, as if she didn't dare to breathe. But Kathy sat up straighter and looked Onkel Franz in the eye. "Franz, I see no harm in letting Maria go to the candy store with her friends once in a while after school. She gets so lonely here, and we—"

Onkel Franz suddenly bolted upward, fury twisting his face. He threw his knife onto the plate with a clatter and bellowed, "I—I, not you—am her guardian! It is my job to decide! *Mine!*"

Kathy's eyes widened in shock, and for a moment she was tongue-tied. Not easily cowed, though, she tried again. "Franz, Maria needs—"

"*No!* And furthermore—" Suddenly, he dropped his voice as if realizing that shouting was beneath him. "Furthermore, *Maria*"—he spat her name as if it were poison—"you will no longer attend Mass. You will stay home instead and read books that I provide for you."

"Franz!" Tante Elisabeth gasped in horror. "You can't mean that!"

"No more!" Onkel Franz swiped at the air with his arm, as if wiping the Catholic Church out of existence. "No more ever! I will not have Maria's mind being filled with ridiculous superstitions and fairy tales!"

"But Franz," came Anni's timid voice, "Maria is a Roman Catholic just as we are. Karl—well, all of us really—raised her that way, and he would want that to continue. She must go to Mass. Every Catholic must!"

Onkel Franz looked around the dining room dramatically. "Do you *see* Karl anywhere?" he sneered. "Do you see His Holiness or your priest hiding in the shadows? I don't . . . so *I* will oversee her religious education from now on. Besides, if Karl had been worried about it, why did he choose me as her guardian? I have never been a good Catholic—or cared about religion."

"Why would he doubt your faith," asked Anni bitterly, "when even I didn't know you had none? Why did you pretend to be a Catholic all this time, Franz, if you believe none of it?"

Onkel Franz sat down and picked up his roll and

knife again. "You wanted a church wedding, my dear," he responded carelessly, as if that explained everything. Anni gazed at him in shock, her eyes filling with tears.

"Pfft, Maria doesn't need Mass," continued Onkel Franz. "I promise you, I will teach her all she needs to know about God."

The dining room was silent as Onkel Franz ate another bite of his roll. The women and Maria exchanged bewildered glances. Finally, Kathy ventured, "How . . . how will you teach her? And what?"

Without answering, Onkel Franz took a sip of his beer and shoveled a huge bite of *Tafelspitz* into his mouth.

Tante Elisabeth spoke up boldly, her worry overtaking her fear of Onkel Franz' temper. "Franz, what will you teach her about God without the Church to guide you?"

Onkel Franz didn't look up. He only smiled to himself and chewed. At last he flicked his eyes upward to meet Tante Elisabeth's. "Nothing," he calmly replied. "And neither will you."

At first, Anni was certain her loving, new husband wasn't serious. "After all," she reasoned to Maria, Kathy, and Tante Elisabeth when Onkel Franz went out later that evening, "he has never tried to talk me out of my faith or keep me home from Mass. Perhaps he has just had a bad week and was overly tired."

Everyone could see the logic in this, so on Sunday

morning, Maria dressed for Mass as usual and put on her coat. Then she followed Kathy, Anni, and Tante Elisabeth out the door as she always did when they left for Mass.

"Wait," came Onkel Franz' calm voice behind them. "Maria, you will stay home with me."

All of them stopped, turning in dismay to see Onkel Franz standing with his arms crossed at the door, his face stony. Maria tried to take Tante Elisabeth's hand, but gently she pushed Maria toward the house. "No, Gusti," she said softly. "I think it's best that you obey your uncle right now. Read your Bible storybook this morning, and I will pray for guidance."

Reluctantly, Maria returned to the house, where Onkel Franz motioned for her to sit on the sofa. Slowly, she tucked her skirt underneath her and sat down on her hands, wanting more than anything to disappear from his piercing gaze. With her eyes fixed firmly on the floor, she waited, her heart beating wildly. Still, Onkel Franz said nothing; he only stood and watched her.

The silence of the house grew louder and louder in his unfriendly presence. Why did he not say anything? Was he waiting for her to speak? Perhaps that was it, she thought.

"Um . . . Onkel Franz, may I get a book to read?" she asked timidly, glancing up at him to be polite and then quickly back down at the floor. If she could read her Bible storybook, as Tante Elisabeth had suggested, it would be a little like going to Mass.

Onkel Franz gave a curt nod and motioned toward the stairs. Maria hurried up the stairs, but on the fourth step, he suddenly called out, "Wait! Come back and sit down. You have given me an idea."

Maria slowly returned to the sofa, wondering what he had in mind now.

Onkel Franz was reaching into the bookcase near his chair by the fireplace. He pulled out a small red book and held it out to her. "Here," he said, "you may read this."

Maria turned it over and read the cover: *Mythical Gods and Heroes of Ancient Greece*. She looked at Onkel Franz, bewildered.

"There, your new church," he said, a note of triumph in his voice, and walked away.

Maria stared at the book, imagining Tante Elisabeth, Kathy, and Anni at Mass without her. It didn't feel right, she thought. She should be there, too, praying with them and breathing in the fragrant incense and watching the priest raise the Precious Body and Blood high above the altar. Why wouldn't Onkel Franz let her go? It didn't hurt him any. But the house remained silent, and all she could do was sit there, hoping that everyone would return soon.

That morning was the longest of her life, but Onkel Franz was just getting started in his new role as guardian.

The next afternoon after school, Maria came home right away, just as she usually did. Yet Onkel Franz met her at the back door with a fierce scowl.

"You stayed late playing with your friends, didn't you?" he growled as she sidled past him.

Maria shook her head, looking around anxiously for a sign of Tante Elisabeth or Kathy. "No, Onkel Franz, I promise I didn't. I came right home."

Onkel Franz slammed the door shut and grabbed her by the arm. Pulling her close, he studied her face, as if trying to decide whether she were lying. Maria gasped in pain and tried to look away, but Onkel Franz grabbed her chin and forced her to look at him. Finally, he let go. "See that you come home immediately *every* day. I will know if you don't; you can be sure of that. I am watching you, Maria, just as your father wanted me to."

Maria rubbed her throbbing chin and backed away. Anger flared within her at the mention of Father. How badly she wanted to retort that he would have never wanted Onkel Franz to treat her this way, but she didn't dare. Instead, she hurried to her room, hoping he would leave her alone for the rest of the day.

Because of his job downtown, Onkel Franz was gone every morning when Maria woke up for school. Tante Elisabeth and Kathy gave her a bowl of muesli or a plate filled with a roll, butter, apricot jam, and sometimes a boiled egg, and they talked of happy things as usual.

Before she left for school, they prayed the Our Father and the Glory Be together, and Tante Elisabeth asked for God's special blessing upon Maria.

But when Maria returned home from school, Onkel Franz was usually waiting for her now—sometimes by the back door and sometimes in his chair by the fireplace but always with a thin wooden switch in his hand. At first, especially when Tante Elisabeth was working in the kitchen, he only glowered at her or studied her in his calm, stern way with the switch held as if ready to strike. When she and Kathy were gone to the market or other shops around the neighborhood or upstairs in their bedrooms, Onkel Franz was worse. Maria dreaded those days, for it was then that Onkel Franz frightened her most.

"You are late today! You skipped school and went downtown!" he began to shout the moment she walked through the door. "I told you I would know. I know everything, and now you will pay!"

If he wasn't accusing her of playing hooky or playing with her friends, Onkel Franz was accusing her of spending the money he gave her for school supplies on cookies and candy. It was never true, so Maria would always shake her head and back away from him, assuring him that she always came home right away as fast as she could. Onkel Franz would act as if she hadn't spoken. Instead, he would grab her and shake her in fury before ordering her up to her room to do her homework that minute—or else! Sometimes, as she ran up the stairs, he would strike her backside with his switch until she was out of reach.

During the evenings, Tante Elisabeth and Kathy spoke more quietly while Maria helped wash the dishes after supper, as if they feared he would hear them. When she was finished, she would hide in her room until bedtime, so that she wouldn't risk making Onkel Franz angry. Sometimes she could hear Anni crying behind her bedroom door across the hall, and she worried about what he might have done or said to her. Anni was gentle and meek and deserved only kindness, but Maria suspected that Onkel Franz had begun to be cruel to her, too.

Weekends were worse. Every Sunday, Maria watched the rest of the family leave for Mass while Onkel Franz ordered her to sit and read any book he believed would pluck out the Catholic faith that Tante Elisabeth had planted in Maria's heart. Sometimes he made her read myths or fairy tales, and other times he would read to her parts of books he liked. They were strange books that Maria didn't understand very well. They said that the best kind of government is a socialist one that forbids religious fantasies and superstitions to be taught to children.

Sometimes, when he was in an especially good mood, Onkel Franz explained what he read to Maria. She tried to understand as best she could, sitting still and quiet so as not to anger him, but she couldn't help starting at every little noise outside in hopes of it being Tante Elisabeth, Kathy, and Anni coming home.

Life went on like this until Maria was nearly thirteen years old. Then, one day in November she came home a half hour later than usual. Frau Koller, her history teacher, had stopped her to discuss the low grade she had earned on her recent test, insisting that she review some of the material with her. Maria tried to tell her she must go right home, but Frau Koller was determined that Maria do better in her class. The moment she was released, Maria fled the school, running home as fast as she could—but it was too late.

"Where have you been?" shouted Onkel Franz when she flew through the back door. Tante Elisabeth jumped where she stood at the kitchen counter, dropping her mixing spoon with a clatter. Maria froze, terrified as he approached her, tall and threatening, his face twisted with rage. Behind him, she could see Kathy peeking around the corner from the living room, her eyes wide.

"Nowhere, Onkel Franz! I promise!" she cried. "Frau Koller made me stay after school to talk about my history test. That's all!"

"Liar!" he shrieked, shaking his switch at her. "I told you I know everything you do. Nothing escapes me! You played with your friends, and now you are lying about it!"

"No, I didn't, Onkel Franz! I didn't!" Maria cried,

cowering against the door with her arms covering her head to protect it from the switch.

Like lightning, he grabbed Maria's arm and pulled her behind him as he marched to the nearest dining room chair.

"Ow!" cried Maria. "That hurts, Onkel Franz!"

Kathy bolted into the dining room, crying, "Stop, Franz!"

"Franz, let go of her!" cried Tante Elisabeth, running to Maria's side. "She is not a liar. If she says Frau Koller talked to her, then that's what happened!"

Onkel Franz threw himself down in the chair and yanked Maria over his knee. "Get away, Elisabeth! I am her guardian, not you. I decide if she's a liar or not, and I say she is! She always lies—and probably steals, too!"

As he raised the switch, Tante Elisabeth pulled at his arm to prevent him from striking her, and Kathy joined her, but Onkel Franz pushed them both away. "Stop interfering, you wretched women! Now you can see what has come of your raising a spoiled brat. This is your fault!"

With that, he brought the switch down hard on Maria's backside—over and over again, as Tante Elisabeth wept. Kathy wrung her hands for a moment and then tried to stop his arm again, but she only slowed him down a little.

At first, Maria cried out in pain, but as Onkel Franz

brought his hand down for the eighth time, she suddenly stopped as rage replaced her fear. It flowed through her like a rushing river, powerful and merciless. Gritting her teeth, she fell silent and let the rage consume her as Onkel Franz struck her three more times. When he finally pushed her off his knee, Maria stood quickly to face him, her chin lifted defiantly. She met his eyes without fear, for she was no longer the same meek child she had been a moment ago. It was then that she knew that nothing Onkel Franz did after this could ever hurt her again.

Thrusting his finger into her face, he snarled, "Don't you ever be late again after school, or this is what will happen from now on—every time. I will not raise a lying brat. You will obey me!"

Maria glared back him without flinching. As Tante Elisabeth wrapped her in a tearful hug, Maria stood there stiffly, never taking her eyes from Onkel Franz'. Strangely, she felt no pain. She felt nothing except contempt and anger toward this cruel man who had made her life so miserable.

When it seemed as if he was finished with her, Maria turned around without a word and walked out of the dining room with her back straight and her head held high. Slowly, she climbed the stairs, her rattled mind beginning to clear.

"I know what I will do," she decided as she gazed out her bedroom window toward the setting sun. "If I am going to be beaten anyway, I will do everything exactly the way I want to from this day forward. When Onkel Franz tells me to do something I don't want to do, I will do the opposite. If he asks me a question, I will tell him a lie. If he tells me to come home on time, I will be late. If he accuses me of spending time with my friends or buying treats with my supply money, I will do exactly that. I will do exactly what I want, when I want, the way I want, and he will never frighten me again."

The crucifix on her wall caught her eye as a ray of sunlight shifted onto it. Maria stared at it for a moment, her heart waging an unseen battle. Then she walked over to it, took it down, and hid it under her bed.

3

RETURN TO JESUS

April 1923

COULD THERE POSSIBLY BE a more heavenly setting for Bach's *Saint Matthew Passion* than the Jesuit church? Maria thought, gazing up in awe at the richly colored frescoes that spanned the ceiling and the gold engravings that framed each one. How lucky she was to have chanced upon it just as the Palm Sunday Mass was about to start! What did it matter if the crowd of worshipers crushed her so hard that she could barely move, let alone stand comfortably? If she fainted, no one would know because she couldn't fall down. She nearly laughed out loud at this thought. Well, at least it wasn't hot in the church, or standing for the whole Mass would be unbearable.

The line of priests and altar boys stood attentively at the back of the church, so it wouldn't be long before the *Passion* would begin. If only they could skip all the ceremony and liturgy and just play the music! Maria thought longingly of the stairs she had passed on her way into the church. Usually, whenever she had a chance to hear a Mass featuring the music of the great composers or the singing of the Vienna Boys' Choir, she would sit on any stairs she could find, such as those of a side altar, and face the wall so that she could forget everything but the music. The Mass itself meant nothing to her, but ah, the music! Now, though, she had no choice but to stand with the crowd and hope the music was well worth the discomfort she would have to endure.

Suddenly, she yelped as the high-heeled shoe of the woman in front of her came down hard on her right foot. The woman quickly turned around to apologize, but an angry jab came just as quickly into her left ribs.

"Shh!"

Maria turned to glare at the indignant elderly woman beside her. "She stepped on my foot," explained Maria coldly without bothering to whisper.

The elderly woman ignored her, instead placing her finger against her lips and scowling fiercely at Maria. "Shh! You are being disrespectful, young lady!"

Maria glared at the woman harder and then snapped her head to the front with a sassy flick of one of her long brown braids. As she did so, she saw that the processional had begun, so she quickly composed herself and waited in anticipation for the beautiful strains of Bach's music to lift her soul to heaven—or at least the ceiling, since as far as she was concerned heaven wasn't real.

Except there was no Bach. There was nothing but a droning Gregorian chant to accompany the procession down the aisle. Maria groaned in disappointment and frustration. They always played the *Saint Matthew Passion* on Palm Sunday! Why did they change it? And now what was she supposed to do? Standing for an hour and listening to a boring priest wasn't the way she wanted to spend the beautiful March morning.

She twisted her head to locate the nearest door and quickly gave up. She couldn't see anything with the crowd of people behind her. The door was a long walk from where she stood, and there was no way to get there without causing a disruption. Although she didn't care much about distracting people from their worship, she did care about drawing attention to herself and making more people angry. No, there was nothing for it, she realized. She would have to stay where she was and just hope the real music would begin later.

Crossing her arms in annoyance, she sighed and let her mind roam as the priest led the congregation through the long prayers and Scripture readings before he finally climbed the stairs to the raised pulpit to deliver the homily. Ah, she realized with a grudging respect, it's Father Kronseder. She hadn't heard him say Mass before, but she recognized him from pictures and articles, for he was quite well known for his powerful homilies. Perhaps, just this once, she would pay attention so that she could say she had heard the great man speak.

"Two thousand years ago today," Father Kronseder began, his voice clear and full of emotion, "our Lord rode into Jerusalem on a humble donkey—*our* Lord . . . *our* King . . . *our* Savior. The one who was present at the creation of the universe, the earth, and all that is in it. The sacrificial lamb who would save us all from the price we deserved to pay for our sins, the eternal pains of hell. *This* day marked the beginning of the end when He would suffer unimaginable tortures and ultimately die in *our* place because of His everlasting, unfathomable love for us—and not just die, but die in the worst way possible in the first-century Roman Empire: by crucifixion."

The rest of the homily passed in a blur for Maria as she listened, transfixed by the power of the priest's moving words on Christ's Passion. After the homily, as Father Kronseder consecrated the Eucharist, Maria's mind began to whirl. What had she just heard? Could it possibly be true? Did this man—and he was just a man, she reminded herself—really believe all these outlandish things that he was preaching to the hundreds of trusting Catholics gazing up at him? How could someone so obviously brilliant be so foolish, so stupid? After all, he had given up his whole life to this Jesus of whom he spoke so passionately, surrendering a career, female love and companionship, children, and even a home of his own. What a waste of a life it was to dedicate one's brilliance to fairy tales and superstitions! Wasn't it? Maria was baffled, and for the first time in years, she felt a twinge of uncertainty about her conviction that the Resurrection of Jesus was mere fantasy.

When the Mass was finally over, Maria stood for a moment where she was, anxious to leave as quickly as possible but still moved by the beauty and power of Father Kronseder's homily. Presently, she noticed him climb the stairs to the pulpit again to retrieve something. Ha, this was her chance to deal with this nonsense once and for all! Scoffing with a loud "Tsk!", she marched toward the pulpit. The moment he descended the stairs again, she blocked his path with her arms crossed.

"Do you really believe all that?"

Father Kronseder stared down at her in surprise. "All what, my child?"

Maria straightened and looked him impudently in the eye. "All that you said in your homily. Everything!"

The aging priest smiled kindly at Maria and took her

gently by the arm. "Let's go in here to talk," he said as he guided her into the sacristy nearby. Then he turned to her and asked, "Don't you believe it, my child?"

"Of course not!" responded Maria, wondering at the tartness of her own voice. After all, she wanted to understand him, not belittle him. "Of course not," she repeated more gently. "I am from the State Teachers College of Progressive Education." She couldn't help adding a note of pride to her statement, for the college had in recent years become a model of socialism, which was the modern form of Austrian government. It was happily free from any Church influence.

Father Kronseder nodded knowingly. "Ah," he said. He glanced at his wristwatch and seemed to be thinking carefully. "I'm very sorry. I must be at the university in a quarter of an hour, but on Tuesday at four I'll have time to chat and I will be waiting to see you. Good-bye for now!" At that, he walked out of the sacristy, leaving Maria to watch him go in bewilderment.

For the rest of the afternoon, Maria agonized over what to do. She had been looking forward to a class ski trip next week. All her friends were to leave together on Monday and ski some of the best slopes in the Alps. She had been looking forward to it for weeks, and now one of the most famous theologians in the country was expecting her to show up in his office on Tuesday to answer her questions about God. He hadn't even given her a chance to tell him she had plans!

Maria left the church slowly and was immediately

blinded by the brilliant sunlight outside. She stopped to let her eyes adjust.

Paul. The name edged its way into her mind as she stood there, and after a moment she remembered that in her childhood Bible storybook, Paul was the apostle who had hated Christians so much that he tried to kill them all. Then, one day, he was blinded by a light from heaven, and the voice of Jesus spoke to him. At that moment he came to believe in Jesus, and he spent the rest of his life preaching the Gospel to everyone who would listen.

As she trudged down the street deep in thought, Maria frowned as she reminded herself how silly Catholics were. The Bible's account of Paul was a lie like all the rest of it. It was just a made-up story—either that, or Paul was an imaginative fool. And what a fool Father Kronseder was, too, for that matter. Of course, she had to show up for him on Tuesday, ski trip or no ski trip! She couldn't let him think he had won, that she was afraid to hear what he had to say. No, she had to put him in his place by showing him how mistaken he and every other priest was for wasting their lives preaching about a God who didn't exist and about the man named Jesus, who died and stayed dead like anyone else. Onkel Franz and the Austrian school system had taught her well. Perhaps now it was her mission to help her fellow Austrians see the truth and free them from the lies of religion!

For the next two days, Maria planned all the things

she would say to Father Kronseder. She certainly had plenty to get off her chest. He would sit there staring at her in shock, coming to his senses with a sudden realization of his errors. He wouldn't have any response at all, but Maria would wait patiently, just to be fair. Finally—she could just picture it!—she would stand up with a smug smirk on her face, say "I thought so. Good day, Father Kronseder," and walk out his door with her head held high and with him crouched low in his chair in utter humiliation. The more she thought about it, the more she couldn't wait!

～

With an almost giddy anticipation, Maria knocked on Father Kronseder's office door at four o'clock sharp on Tuesday afternoon. "Come in!" came the reply.

Maria strode into the office boldly. "Good day, Father Kronseder," she greeted him, with what she hoped was a chilly, formal smile.

Father Kronseder returned the smile warmly and beckoned to a chair in front of his desk. "Ah, Fräulein! I wasn't sure I would be seeing you today."

Maria bristled, her mouth stretching into a thin line. "Of course, Father. I had no reason to reject your invitation."

The priest nodded, his smile widening. "I'm so glad. Please, sit down."

Perching on the edge of her chair, Maria stiffened, trying to make herself as tall and imposing as possible. Suddenly, though, she felt a little silly as she thought of her braids and her old brown *Dirndl*, the traditional dress worn in the Austrian Alps. Why hadn't she thought of putting on a blouse and a skirt and wearing her hair up to look older? Next to the distinguished man before her with his tall shelves of books and his polished wooden desk, she felt like an ignorant country girl. Maybe challenging him in matters of theology was a mistake.

"So, Fräulein . . . ?" He paused with a quizzical look.

"Maria," she supplied curtly.

"Maria," he repeated. "On Sunday, you asked me if I believe what I preached. Is that really what you wanted to know?"

"Um . . ." Taken off guard at this unexpected beginning, Maria thought for a moment. She realized that she already knew he believed it. The way he had preached on Sunday with such passion and conviction . . . there was no doubt in her mind. So, what *was* her real question?

The kindly priest gazed at her curiously. "Why didn't you like what I said in my homily?"

All of Maria's carefully prepared words came back to her with a rush. This she could answer! Feeling more confident, she looked Father Kronseder in the eye and began, "There are so many reasons, sir . . . Father. You preached to hundreds of trusting people that we are all sinners bound for hell without Jesus' atoning death on the cross. Do you know how silly and un-Austrian that sounds? Who really knows if there is a God? You cannot prove it. He certainly never did anything for me," she added bitterly, the sting of Onkel Franz' cruelty ever present in her heart.

"Oh?" asked Father Kronseder, placing the tips of his fingers together beneath his chin. "What do you mean by that?"

Maria's eyes flashed as a sudden wave of anger flooded her. "I grew up in a home where I was happy and loved. Then when I was nine a cruel man entered my life and made me miserable. He was taken to an insane asylum not too long ago, so now all his wickedness makes at least some sense, but he certainly took away any reason I had to believe in God! Besides, in school my teachers made it very plain that smart, intelligent people have no need of God. And do you know what? They're right —and so was my uncle."

"Why is that?"

Now Maria had her chance to set the good priest straight, to show him how he and the entire Catholic Church were wrong and stuck in medieval ideas. For the next two hours she poured out everything she had been taught about the strengths of atheism and the foolishness of Christianity. Father Kronseder sat in silence, listening in rapt attention until Maria's gush of words slowed to a trickle and finally stopped. When no more words would come, she slumped against the back of her chair and closed her eyes.

How tired she was now. She hadn't planned to say all that. It had just . . . come. And now that it was over, she didn't feel triumphant as she thought she would. She just felt empty and lost and oddly as if everything she had just said was itself a big lie. Wearily, she dropped her head into her hands and sighed.

"Well, my dear," Father Kronseder said, "you have simply been wrongly informed. It sounds to me as if you just need to do some reading. Learning a few things will set you straight." He took a piece of paper from a small stack on his desk and scribbled a few words. "I suggest that you start with this one." He handed it to her and then asked, as if the thought had just occurred to him, "You're Catholic, aren't you?"

Maria snapped her head up and glared at him fiercely. After all she had just said, how could he ask her such a thing?

He smiled in understanding and reworded his question. "When you fill out forms, what religion do you put down for yourself?"

"Well . . . ," Maria responded uncertainly, "I put . . . Roman Catholic . . . I guess. I was baptized. But I have already told you it's all lies."

"Did you leave the Church?"

"No, I'm just . . . not in it."

"It is nearly Easter, Fräulein, so if you haven't left the Church, then it is time for you to do your Easter duty. When did you make your last confession?"

Maria stared at him, barely able to follow this turn of the conversation. "I've never made a confession."

"Then shall this be your first one?"

After Maria nodded the priest asked, "Were you fully informed about Church doctrine by the people who told you it was lies?"

Maria considered. "Well . . . no, I never did learn much beyond Bible stories."

"Are you willing to learn and overcome your ignorance of Christ and His Church?"

"If I've been taught wrongly, as you say, then . . . yes, I am."

"Have you ever been aware of your sins and shortcomings?"

"Well . . . yes," Maria replied shamefacedly. "I was my teachers' nightmare all through upper grade school. I often felt terrible about it, only I could never stop. And I lied and disobeyed all the time at home."

"Are you sorry for what you've said and done that has hurt your teachers and family?"

Maria thought of the many people she had hurt with rude and unkind words since the night Onkel Franz had first beaten her. How obnoxious she had been to them —and none of them had deserved it. Now tears began to flow with true remorse. "Yes. Yes, I wish I could take it all back and do everything differently, but I am almost graduated from college now, you see. It is too late to fix any of it."

"Will you make amends by returning to Christ and the Church, accepting His forgiveness, and seeking a life of holiness from this point forward?"

Maria was silent as she wiped her eyes. She swallowed hard and closed her eyes to focus on the question. After all her years of lying and badgering people to get what she wanted, she wanted to be truthful now—not only to Father Kronseder but also to herself. Was God watching her, waiting for her to turn back to Him? If Jesus really had sacrificed Himself for her so that she could live for eternity in heaven, why not accept this gift?

With a deep breath, Maria nodded and lifted her eyes to meet the old priest's. "Yes, sir. I will."

Father Kronseder leaned toward her, his eyes filled with kindness. "Then take courage, my child. I am going to pronounce the words of absolution. When I do, God will simply erase your sins. They will be no more, and He will forget them completely. Your soul will look like the soul of a newly baptized child."

Maria smiled, her eyes clouding with fresh tears, and waited humbly. As the priest made the sign of the cross before her and said, "*Ego te absolvo*," the sun moved into the window behind him and lit up his white hair like a halo. Maria gazed at him in awe, her heart moved with joy.

Then he stood up and held out his hand to her. Dazed, Maria stood and shook his hand. "Congratulations," he said with a smile. "Nothing can happen to you now. You are all right. Go in peace, my child."

Maria hardly knew what happened after that—how she left his office, how she made her way out of the building, or how she walked straight into an oncoming streetcar, until several hands were around her, pulling her up to a sitting position and checking her head and arms for bruises.

"Are you all right, Fräulein?" asked the young man who had helped her up. "Do you need a doctor?"

"I think she's all right," said another man's voice behind her. "I don't see any blood."

"She didn't get knocked out," said a woman as she smoothed Maria's dress and straightened her coat. "That's a good sign."

Maria smiled wanly, rubbing her head where it had banged into the streetcar. "Yes, I think I'm all right. Thank you all. I don't know what I was thinking."

And with that, Maria fainted into the arms of the young man.

Once she had been revived and returned to college in a taxi by a kind stranger, Maria quickly recovered and plunged into her new life in Christ with a zeal she had never felt before. Without delay she read the book Father Kronseder recommended, understood where she had been misled by Onkel Franz and her teachers, and set about trying to make amends for all the damage she had done to others. She shared the Gospel and the beauty of the Church with everyone who would listen.

By graduation only a few weeks later, she had re-learned everything she had forgotten after Onkel Franz entered her life, and was attending Mass as often as she possibly could. Now she could not learn the beautiful traditions of the Church fast enough or spend enough time in prayer. Where she was obnoxious to her elders before, now she bit her tongue every time she was tempted to say something she shouldn't. She studied hard, received her teaching degree, and left college with a renewed commitment to honor Jesus in her new profession in every way that she could. Nothing else mattered now. Her soul was healed.

~

"Oh Gustl, isn't it beautiful?"

Maria's friend Kathrin paused to set down her knapsack and sip from her canteen, her eyes taking in the vista before them. Maria followed her gaze to the rich, green valley that spread far below. Nestled between two mountains, the village in the valley lay content in the warm June sunshine, as if nothing in the world could threaten its peace.

"Hear that?" Maria asked, hitching the coiled rope on her shoulder a little higher.

They stood silently, listening. "The evening bells at the church," said Kathrin softly, not wanting to speak above the joyful, musical clanging that rose from the village below like laughter. "Oh Gustl, the world is such a magical place sometimes, isn't it?"

Maria smiled. "That it is. On days like this, it just fills my heart with joy! It smells like summer up here, too. But everyone's far ahead now, so we'd better hurry to catch up."

It wasn't long before they reached the rest of the girls, who were trudging up the steep incline just ahead. Maria took up the rear of the hiking party because she was the most experienced, as well as the handiest with the ice pick and rope. All of them were well-seasoned hikers as most Austrians were, and it was not uncommon to see groups of young people hiking or camping along the trails for days at a time. This trip was to last several days, in fact, as a celebration of their recent graduation from college. Soon they would all scatter into their new lives as teachers, but right now was their time to be young and free and to rejoice in the beauty of their homeland. To Maria nothing could possibly be better. Perhaps, she thought, as the group turned downward toward an enormous glacier, she should be a professional mountain guide instead of a teacher.

As she mulled this idea over in her mind, the group approached the glacier, which lay sparkling in the setting sun. The trail wound around it before dipping down to the village. Near the dip, however, another trail branched off to follow the ridge across to the next mountain. Maria scanned the trail where it disappeared over a hill on the other side of the glacier. Just before the hill stood a grove of evergreen trees that seemed like a promising shelter from any wind that might whip up during the night. They really should set up camp soon. Although they weren't very high and the girls were all experts at camping, night fell quickly in the mountains. They would need all the light available to pitch their tents and cook supper.

"Let's make camp over there," called Maria, pointing to the trees. The other girls called back their agreement and followed the trail around the glacier. Everyone was weary from the day's hike, and Maria's back ached from carrying all her gear. Thankfully she would soon be able to eat something and crawl inside her cozy sleeping bag to giggle away an hour or so with her friends. That was her favorite part of hiking!

Never had Maria felt so alive than at this moment, for as the sun continued to set, it seemed to set fire to the glacier, transforming it into a medallion of burnished gold and magenta. Maria stopped to absorb the beauty around her, her senses buzzing with a joy that seemed too much to bear. Above the glacier the sky was awash in purple, rose, and orange, and the evening star appeared above the trees on the other side, shimmering like a queen's diamond.

"Oh God," Maria gasped, overcome by emotion. "Oh God, *You* made all of this. You and only You, for

You are the Great Artist. Mankind can create nothing —nothing!—compared with this."

Slowly, she turned in a circle, drinking in the snowy peaks rising above her, the fertile valley below, the brilliant sunset, and the fiery glacier. It was all too, too much!

Suddenly, Maria flung her arms wide. "Oh Jesus, You gave me everything! There is nothing I could want that You do not provide. You are Love, You are Beauty, You are Light! What can I give you, Jesus? What can you possibly want from me?"

Maria stilled her mind, thinking deeply. She hardly heard the calls of her friends, who had now reached the other side of the glacier. Surely she had something she could offer Jesus in return for His unfailing love. How could she show Him the same kind of sacrificial love He had shown her? She must give up something —something that she loved and cherished, something that would hurt to surrender.

Her eyes fell upon the church steeple far below in the valley, and then it came to her. She loved hiking, sports, and the outdoors almost more than anything else in the world, so she would surrender that. She would surrender it so completely that she would never even get an opportunity to change her mind. Instead, she would enter the dark and cloistered world of convent life, hidden from the hills and valleys and forests and rivers that she loved. Yes, it was the only way. She would become a nun.

For a moment her heart felt as if it would leap out of her chest as she sensed with certainty that this was the answer she was looking for. *This* was her calling, and she had to respond right now. She couldn't wait whole days to give Jesus this part of her life. How could she hike and laugh and gossip with the other girls when Jesus would be kept waiting?

Glancing toward the low-hanging sun and then down to the valley, she gauged whether she had enough light to make it down before it was dark. Yes, she could do it. She *had* to do it. If she hurried, she could make it down in a half hour and catch the last train to nearby Salzburg. There were several convents there that she could visit in the morning. Even if it did get completely dark before she made it down the mountain, she had her flashlight.

Suddenly, her feet took wings, and she nearly ran to catch up with her friends. As she approached them near the campsite, she called out, "I have to go, everyone! I need to get back to Salzburg right now!"

The other girls looked at her as if she had taken leave of her senses. "Now?" asked Kathrin. "Why now? It's almost dark. What's the matter?"

Maria was too excited to chat. "Nothing's the matter! Nothing at all!" She laughed and rushed to each one of her friends, wrapping them in quick hugs. "Everything's absolutely wonderful. I just need to get back. I can't explain right now, but I promise I'll tell you all about it later. You won't believe it! But now I must hurry down to the train."

Trotting past the grove of trees toward the village trail on the other side, she waved back at them. "I promise I'll write you all very soon. It will make sense; you'll see! Have a wonderful time on the rest of the hike! I love you all!"

"But Maria!" they cried after her. "Wait; don't go!"

"I promise!" she called once more, and blew them kisses until the trail carried her out of their sight.

Maria had never descended a trail as quickly as she did now. At times she nearly slipped onto her backside as rocks dropped away from her hiking boots, but she was a sturdy hiker. The sunset transformed into black velvet, and from time to time the lights of nearby cottages twinkled through the trees, as if to assure Maria that she didn't have far to go. It wasn't long before Maria found herself on the village streets again, winding her way to the train depot. Two hours later, she had found an inexpensive inn in the beautiful city of Salzburg and was sleeping more deeply than she had in months. Tomorrow, she thought as she drifted off to sleep. Tomorrow she would start her new life. It was only a matter of where.

Indeed, when she found herself out on the bustling streets again the next morning, she stood perplexed for a few moments, for she wasn't sure which convent she should try first. It couldn't just be any convent, she decided. If she was going to give her whole life to God as a nun, she wanted to do it completely. She must find the strictest convent in town. But which one was that?

Just ahead at an intersection, she saw a policeman directing traffic. Hmm, she thought. Perhaps he would know.

Striding up to him, she said, "Excuse me, Herr Policeman."

The policeman turned to her with a slight frown. After all, he was rather busy. "Yes, Fräulein?"

"Can you please tell me, where is the strictest convent in town?"

The policeman stared at her, baffled. "The strictest con—well, my dear, I surely don't know that myself." He scratched his head, scanning the streets as if a convent might be hiding among the shops and cafés nearby. Then he brightened. "Ah! That man coming our way looks like a monk. Ask him."

Maria turned to see a youngish man wearing the robes of a Capuchin monk approaching the intersection. The policeman spoke for her.

"Good day, Brother," he greeted the man. "This *junge Dame* has a question you might be able to answer."

The monk looked even more baffled than the policeman had. "Yes?"

"She wonders if you might know which convent in the city is the strictest?"

Wrinkling his brow in thought, the monk considered for a moment. "Well, I believe that would be Nonnberg Abbey. They are well known for their austere way of life."

"Yes, Nonnberg!" agreed the policeman. "Of course. Fräulein, that is behind you about a half mile. If you follow this road, you will see a sign for Nonnberg before long."

Maria smiled at the two men and thanked them. Then, hitching up her ice pick, coil of rope, and knapsack once more, she threaded her way through the busy morning crowd back the way she had come. Sure enough, after a few minutes, a small sign pointed the way to Nonnberg Abbey down a side street.

The abbey's doors were enormous and made of glossy, dark wood. Large iron rings hung from them as handles, and a bell cord hung down in front of the door. Maria stood before the door, flooded with anxiety for the first time. Was this really the best way she could serve God? Had she really felt a call to surrender everything she loved? And what if the convent said no?

Then she remembered the glacier and her determination to give God everything. Surely, she thought, if this wasn't God's will, He would show her what to do. After all, as Tante Elisabeth had told her long ago, He would always be with her. She had forgotten that for a long time, but now she was determined never to forget again. She must trust God.

Straightening to her full height, Maria rang the bell cord and waited. After several minutes the door finally creaked slowly open to reveal a tiny, white-haired nun with a large cross around her neck. Her blue eyes gleamed with kindness and gentleness, and Maria immediately felt at ease.

"Good day," Maria said in as friendly a tone as she could manage. "I have come to join you here. I would like to be a nun."

If the old nun was as baffled as the policeman and monk had been, she didn't show it. Her wrinkles only deepened as she beamed at Maria. "Is that right, my child?" she asked. Her eyes took in the ice pick and rope and flickered for an instant. Maria cleared her throat in embarrassment, as she realized how ridiculous she must look. Perhaps she should have prepared a little better, she thought. She didn't know much about nuns, but she was pretty sure they had no use for ice picks and climbing ropes. The nun didn't seem to mind, though. "And who sent you here?" she asked gently.

Maria snorted. "Sent me? I assure you, Frau . . . Sister . . . if someone had sent me, I wouldn't be here. I haven't obeyed anybody yet!"

The nun gazed at her a moment, her eyes narrowing a bit as they studied Maria's earnest face. Finally, she nodded and opened the door wider. "I see. Then welcome to Nonnberg Abbey, my child. Come in."

So Maria hitched her knapsack and rope high on her shoulders one more time and stepped through the abbey door.

4

COMING HOME TO AIGEN

June 1925

C HILDREN, I HAVE GOOD NEWS. I have finally found
a lovely new house for us near Salzburg!"

Georg von Trapp scanned the faces of his seven children as they gaped at him in shocked silence. Then
he realized his mistake. Rupert and Agathe, being the
oldest at ages thirteen and twelve, had known his plans
for a while, but he had forgotten that the other five

children had no idea yet. He cleared his throat nervously and stood up. Suddenly, he felt too warm there in the sitting room as the sunset cast its mellow light into every corner. Removing his cotton sweater, he laid it on the easy chair. All words had flown from his head, so he began to pace.

"Papa?" Hedwig, seven years old, prompted him from where she sat on the couch reading "The Shoemaker and the Elves" to four-year-old Martina.

Georg cleared his throat again and stopped pacing to face the children. "Yes . . . well . . ." His eyes lit upon the framed portrait of a woman, also named Agathe, that graced the fireplace mantel. He walked over to it and picked it up, for a moment lost in his sorrow for his beautiful wife. Running his fingers lightly over the photograph, he said wistfully, "It's been three years since Mama died."

"Yes, Papa, come September it will be," said Rupert from the other side of the room, a soft cloth suspended from one hand. He had been cleaning his accordion. Georg had started teaching him only a few months ago, and he was learning quickly.

Georg gently placed the portrait where it belonged and continued. "As you all know, I miss Mama very much, and it has been hard for me to get used to life without her. Hard for all of us, of course. I think that it's time now for us to start a new adventure—not so that we forget Mama but so that we can do some new things and make some new friends. This house has become too sad for me." He cast his eyes around the cozy room, which Agathe had decorated herself, and his heart twisted painfully. "So, I have bought a new house for us in Aigen, which is in the country just outside Salzburg. It's a beautiful house, big enough for all of us, as well as all the servants."

"Salzburg?" asked five-year-old Johanna. "Where's that?"

"Oh, you remember," Agathe reminded her. "It's where Mama took us to the dentist sometimes."

"Ohhhh," said Johanna, her face screwed up with the effort of remembering. "I don't think Mama took me there."

"Probably not, dear one," said Georg with a smile. "You were too little. But Salzburg is a lovely city, full of music and light and elegance. I think you will all like it there."

"When do we move, Papa?" piped up ten-year-old Mitzi from her favorite cozy chair, where she had been dressing her doll.

Georg smiled, pleased that his children seemed at ease with the news. "At the end of June," he said.

"But that's this month!" cried nine-year-old Werner.

Georg gave a decisive nod and clasped his hands behind his back. "Yes, it's only three weeks from now. We—and all the servants—will have a lot to do. Can I count on you to help?"

Now the children were excited. Three weeks until they would move into a beautiful new house in

Salzburg! "Yes!" they all promised. A grand adventure was just what the von Trapp family needed. They could hardly wait!

~

The family had moved twice before in the children's memory but never to their own house. During the Great War, when Papa had command of a submarine in the Austrian Navy, they had lived with Mama's mother at her mountain farm on Zeller Lake. When the war was finally over in 1918, Mama's brother Franky offered his unoccupied house a half mile away until Papa and Mama could find a suitable house to buy. A year and a half later, the house flooded when a nearby glacier melted, so Papa and Mama moved the family to their current home. It was an unoccupied estate of another of Mama's brothers, Bobby.

Named Martinschlossl, the estate was in Klosterneuburg near Vienna, and everyone loved living there. The children had plenty of room to play, and the family was able to grow its own vegetables and fruit. The von Trapps even kept a cow for milk and cheese. But just before Christmas 1921, the dark shadow of scarlet fever sickened Rupert, Mitzi, Werner, Hedwig, and Martina. Mama nursed them all but contracted the disease herself in January. By September 1922 the symptoms had weakened her so much that the disease claimed her life. Now the beautiful estate was a place of sadness. They had all tried to be happy and move forward as Mama would have wanted, but it just wasn't the same without her cheerful, loving presence. So, when the children first saw their new house from the train windows as the locomotive slowly chugged into the station, they could hardly contain their excitement.

"That's it, children," said Georg, pointing to the back of a pale-yellow mansion winking through the trees in the distance.

The children were on their feet the instant the train screeched to a stop.

"Hurry, let's go!" they cried impatiently. "Come on! Hey, there's Franz and Marie!"

"Wait for me, children!" called Georg as they scampered down the steps and onto the platform.

Franz and Marie Stiegler, who had been the family's caretakers for many years, were at the station with a wooden cart to transport the children's luggage to the house. Georg had already spent several days there to prepare for the children's arrival while they stayed with their cousins at Goldegg Castle outside Sankt Pölten. He smiled at their enthusiasm and hoped they would like their new home as much as he did. It was just what they needed after the past three years of living at Martinschlossl without Mama.

After greeting the Stieglers, Mitzi scanned the road for an entrance to the house. "How do we get there?" she asked, puzzled by the tracks that lay between the station and the long fence that bordered the estate.

Georg placed his hand gently on her shoulder. "Follow Franz and Marie, and you will see."

Once the children's luggage was piled high on the cart, Franz pushed the cart ahead of them out the front door of the station and along the road. They had gone just a short distance when Marie turned toward the tracks and started picking her way across them. Franz followed with the cart more slowly, while Georg helped him from the other side.

"Come, children!" She beckoned to them. "The train won't leave for another few minutes. It's safe."

Quickly, everyone crossed the tracks to the fence that lay beyond. At first it looked as if Marie were going to climb the fence, but then she reached over it and unlatched a little gate. It was through this that the family entered their new home.

The gate opened into a large, shady garden webbed with paths and filled with flowers and bushes of many kinds. The roses, magenta and pale yellow, were now in full bloom. As the family followed the cart along a narrow path toward the mansion, admiring the lovely garden, Georg pointed to the various features of the estate.

"All of this right here, as you can see, is the garden. You may play here anytime," he said. He pointed to the south side of the garden, which lay to their right. "Over there, where you see that small meadow and woods, is also our property. But on the other side of the woods is another estate, so do not go past them."

Pointing to the north side of the garden, he said, "On that side you can see our garage, greenhouse, shed, and laundry house, and a vegetable garden is behind the greenhouse. On the other side of that is our apple orchard. Most of the time I think you will want to play here in the garden."

The children gazed in awe at the huge estate. How could this lovely place belong to them? It was like a dream!

"But it's so big, Papa!" cried Rupert in amazement. "Will we raise animals, as we did at the Martinschlossl?"

"Perhaps we will," mused Georg, stroking his mustache thoughtfully. "I haven't thought about that yet. Come, let me show you the front of the house."

As Franz and Marie continued along the path to a servants' entrance, Georg turned onto a different path that led around the north side of the house. The children followed eagerly, anxious to see the front. That was always the grandest part of any house.

They were not disappointed. The yellow stone walls and dark-walnut double doors gleamed in the afternoon sunshine, and the white-trimmed windows sparkled. The black roof swept gently upward, nesting several arched, gabled windows within it. Stately and proud, the facade seemed to promise unforgettable balls and dinner parties to anyone lucky enough to receive an invitation. In front of the house, softening the mansion's imposing grandeur, enormous old trees lined the long driveway that led to the road, their summer-green leaves rustling in the breeze.

"It's beautiful, Papa," said Agathe with a smile, squeezing his hand. "Does it have a name?"

Georg puffed out his chest, for he had chosen the name himself. "It certainly does. I named it after the first house Mama and I built in Pola just after we were married—before the Great War changed everything. Its name is the Villa Trapp. What do you think?"

The children clapped and cheered their approval, and Georg made a mock bow.

"May we go inside?" asked Mitzi.

Georg nodded and opened his mouth to speak, but the children were too anxious to wait to hear his response. Everyone dashed to the front door to try to be the first inside. Even little Martina ran as fast as her legs could carry her, but Papa quickly grabbed her, slung her onto his shoulders, and took off at a gallop as she shrieked in delight.

Werner reached the door first and flung it open. Everyone piled inside and then stopped to stare. Ahead of them was a large hall, painted gleaming white with a vaulted ceiling. Its parquet flooring had been recently polished, so that the children couldn't help slipping a bit as they turned around to get a better look. Next to the front door was a wide staircase that matched the front door. It, too, shone as if freshly polished. Best of all, the banister was as sturdy as it was graceful—perfect for sliding!

"Can we look in all the rooms, Papa?" asked Hedwig, peeking through one of the open doorways.

Georg smiled with an encouraging gesture. "Of

course! This is your home now. Explore a bit. See if you can find your rooms and the nursery, where Martina, Hedwig, and Johanna will sleep. All your rooms are on the second floor, along with the Stieglers' rooms. The other servants' quarters are on the third floor, so I don't want you up there after you see it this once. They need their privacy."

Nothing could be more exciting to the children than exploring their new home and settling into their rooms. This wasn't their grandmother Gromi's house or Onkel Bobby's house or Onkel Franky's house. No, for the first time the house was *theirs*. And it was beautiful and large and elegant with plenty of room for all of them—including the chef, the housekeeper, the two maids, the Stieglers, and the younger children's nanny. At dinner that evening (in their new dining room!), all of them agreed that Papa had picked the perfect house for them. Although Mama would never be far from their thoughts, their new home seemed like a happy place that would soon be full of life and laughter.

And it was. Throughout the summer, the children discovered their favorite places to play, and Georg built a log playhouse near the small woods on the eastern portion of the estate. They sang folk songs together in the sitting room on chilly evenings and played ball or running games on the terrace when the evenings were warm. George bought two cows and a dog, as well as chickens and a goat, and the children enjoyed helping to care for them.

He quickly discovered a problem, however. When the children were playing in the garden or the woods, they couldn't hear him call, for the estate was too large. One night in his study, Georg's eyes lit upon his boatswain's whistle, and he had an idea. The whistle was ear-splittingly loud, designed to be heard by his crew over the crashing sounds of waves and other noises on his ships. Why not give the children their own signals, so that they could hear him wherever they were?

The whistle worked perfectly. The children loved their signals; they liked to imagine themselves as sailors on one of Papa's ships. Best of all, the whistle's piercing sound carried all the way to the back fence, so the children could hear their signals anywhere on the estate.

The summer passed in a whirl of color and delights for the children. For Georg, though, the new life he had begun for his family rang hollow sometimes, despite the charms of Salzburg and the friends he already had nearby. Deep inside, he grieved what he had left behind. On warm evenings he would sometimes sit on the terrace as the children played and think of his lost Agathe, whom he had loved with all his heart. How much she would have loved their new home, he thought wistfully. How much he missed her and wished she could be here to help their young daughters grow up. With a bittersweet smile to himself, he thought of the wonderful years they had shared.

He missed his ship, too. After the Great War, the borders of Austria had shifted, and it had lost its access to the sea—and thus its need for a navy. He was a decorated, landlocked naval captain with seven motherless children and nothing to do but remember. It was times like these, when his heart ached the most, that he wondered with dread what the long years ahead held for him. He loved his children and his new home, and his faith and friends soothed his soul. Thanks to his government income and Agathe's remaining wealth, he also had enough money to sustain the lifestyle expected of a baron. Even so, it didn't feel like enough. Inside he felt sad and empty, but what else was there?

All too soon autumn came and with it, new schools for the older children—Werner and Rupert at the local public school and Mitzi and Agathe at the Ursuline Convent School. Hedwig, Johanna, and Martina remained at home with their nanny and Baroness Mendelsloh, the motherly housekeeper. Without a car, which Georg planned to buy eventually, the walk to school was long—forty-five minutes each way. Still, autumn had its own delights. The von Trapps learned how to keep bees for their honey, and they began to spend more time studying music together in the evenings.

The family's musical evenings were quickly becoming a tradition, in fact. While Rupert, Werner, Agathe, and Mitzi completed their homework, Georg taught

Johanna the violin. As the older children finished, he would work with them on their instruments—Rupert and Mitzi on the accordion, Agathe on the guitar, and Mitzi also on the violin.

Later, just before bedtime, they would all sing together. Papa had begun teaching them old naval songs and funny ballads, along with their favorite Austrian folk songs and hymns. As they sang, he would accompany them on his guitar. Everyone loved making music together, and it helped to while away the long winter hours until spring arrived with its longer hours of daylight. Then they played outdoor games on warm evenings. Music did not fall by the wayside, though, for it had made its way into the family's heart and soul and had become part of every day.

The next spring and summer passed happily, ending with a memorable three-week camping trip for Georg, the oldest four children, and several nearby relatives. Every night, as the weather turned cooler, they all continued their music lessons, learning to sing and play the exquisite music of Austria. With Georg on first violin, Rupert or Mitzi on accordion, Agathe on guitar, and Johanna on second violin, they now had a *Schrammelquartett*, a special type of ensemble in Viennese folk music. At last, though, the summer was over, and school began once again, along with the older children's long walks.

One day in October 1926, Georg happened to glance

out the window of his study to see Agathe and Werner running up the driveway toward the house. Mitzi and Rupert were nowhere to be seen. Concerned, Georg put down his pen and went outside.

"Papa!" gasped Agathe, picking up speed when she saw him. Werner followed close behind.

"Where are Rupert and Mitzi?" he asked. "Is everything all right?"

Agathe and Werner shook their heads but were too out of breath to speak again for a moment. Werner turned and pointed down the driveway. Georg squinted through the trees but couldn't see anything. "They are way back there," Werner said. "Mitzi had to stop a few times. She's having trouble breathing, and she's so tired she can hardly walk."

"Is this the first time this has happened?" asked Georg, his brow furrowed with worry.

"She has been unusually tired for a couple of weeks," replied Agathe, "but she's been keeping up with us. On the way home today, though, she had to stop a few times to rest, and finally Rupert started helping her."

At that moment Rupert and Mitzi appeared at the end of the driveway, and Georg ran to meet them. Rupert was half carrying his sister, and they were both exhausted. Georg took one look at Mitzi's pale, weary face and scooped her into his arms. Gratefully, she leaned her head against his shoulder. "How are you, my darling?" he asked tenderly, as he turned back to the house. "Are you feeling ill?"

Mitzi shook her head. "No, not ill, Papa," she said. "I'm just so tired, and I can't breathe normally."

"When did that begin?"

"I had some trouble all last year, but it wasn't bad enough to say anything. Lately, though, it's been getting worse."

"Do you think we could have bicycles, Papa?" asked Rupert. "Maybe that would be easier for her."

"I've been thinking for a while now about buying you all bicycles to make your trip to and from school easier," replied Georg. "I'll look into it tomorrow. However, a bicycle won't be enough for Mitzi, because you'll still have to walk when it snows. I'll have Dr. Wagner come and examine her. He'll tell us what she needs."

The next morning Agathe, Werner, and Rupert went to school as usual, while Mitzi stayed home. She felt a little better, but she was glad to see Dr. Wagner. She hated being sick, and she missed her friends. If anyone could make her feel better, she was certain, he could.

But Dr. Wagner's remedy turned out to be disappointing. "She cannot return to school, Georg," the doctor said gravely, as he patted Mitzi's arm and stood up. "Not this year, anyway. The heart murmur left by the scarlet fever puts too much strain on her body and has for some time. If I had known she was walking so far to school, I would have said something sooner."

Georg rubbed his forehead, mortified that he hadn't even considered that Mitzi might not be strong enough to walk such a long distance. "Perhaps if I drove her—"

"It isn't just the walk that is causing the fatigue, Georg," interrupted the doctor. "It is also school itself. Sitting there all day, concentrating hour after hour, taking examinations, playing with the other children at recess—all of those things are contributing to the problem."

"What can we do?" asked Georg. "I can hire a governess, but Mitzi wouldn't like being cooped up every day, all day, by herself."

Mitzi looked hopefully at Dr. Wagner. Surely there was some way for her to go to school. Papa was right. Staying home every day with a grouchy old governess would be awful!

Dr. Wagner was firm. "I'm sorry, Georg. Keeping her as quiet and still as possible for the rest of the school year is the only way for her to heal. The best solution is a governess . . . unless, of course, you taught her yourself."

Georg stared at the doctor for a moment, horrified by the idea yet wanting to do the right thing. Then he shook his head. "No, I am quite sure I would ruin such an undertaking. I will find a governess."

Nodding his approval, Dr. Wagner placed his stethoscope into his medical bag and snapped it shut. "I don't know of any possibilities myself, but it is likely that the director at the high school will have some ideas for you." He placed his hand on Georg's shoulder and looked kindly into his eyes. "I know this is distressing, but Mitzi will be all right. A long rest is all she needs to feel like herself again. By summer she'll probably be ready to play outside with the rest of the children. And then next year, perhaps she can return to school."

He turned and gave Mitzi a light tap on the cheek. Smiling down at her, he added, "And see her friends, of course. Missing your friends is what will be hardest for you, I presume."

Mitzi gave him a wan smile, her eyes filling with tears. She nodded.

"Be brave, my girl," Dr. Wagner said. "It won't last forever, and I know your papa will do everything in his power to keep you happy and comfortable." With that, he placed his hat on his head, made a little bow with a click of his heels, and left.

The next morning Georg made an appointment with Herr Lindner, the school director, and met him that afternoon for advice. Perhaps a student about to graduate would be able to tutor Mitzi and also keep up with her own studies, he suggested.

"I'm sorry, Captain von Trapp," said Herr Lindner. "I don't know of any students here that I would feel comfortable recommending. The only governesses and tutors I know who are highly qualified are already engaged with other families."

Georg slumped in his chair, deflated. He rubbed his mustache in frustration. "What about the director of another high school?" he asked. "Do you think any of your colleagues around Salzburg would know of someone?"

Herr Lindner nodded. "Very possibly, and I would be happy to call them and ask. However, an idea has just occurred to me. Recently I heard of a young postulant —twenty-one years old, to be precise—at Nonnberg Abbey whose doctor has recommended a year away from the convent. She has been experiencing constant headaches, and the doctor believes that the confining life of the convent has caused the problem. Before entering the abbey she spent a lot of time outdoors— hiking and biking and that sort of thing—so she was not prepared for the sudden change to a life that is mostly indoors. To live outside the convent for such a long period of time, however, she must have a job to support herself. The abbey cannot provide for her needs for an entire year."

"So she is a high school teacher?"

Herr Lindner shook his head. "No, she teaches the lower grades for the abbey school. However, I understand that she is highly intelligent and an excellent teacher. I'm sure she could adapt to Mitzi's more challenging curriculum. What do you think?"

Georg nodded, feeling hopeful for the first time since Dr. Wagner's visit. "What is her name?"

Herr Lindner began shuffling some papers on his

desk, until he came to the letter he was looking for. "Ah yes, here it is. Her name is Maria Kutschera."

"She sounds like what Mitzi needs," replied Georg. "Would you make the necessary contacts for me?"

Herr Lindner smiled. "I'll do it today and will call you as soon as I know something. If she is agreeable, I will set up an interview for you at your house as well."

"No, no," said Georg. "I can't afford the possibility of losing her to another family. If Nonnberg Abbey approves of her, I'm confident that I will, too. She's hired!"

How wonderfully God had answered his prayer, Georg thought as he left the school. He was encouraged that Mitzi's new governess was named Maria, which was Mitzi's real name. It must be a sign, he thought. She was young, clearly a good Catholic role model, and might have a little sense of fun since she was used to younger children. She didn't even need a permanent job. Both her needs and Mitzi's were only temporary. It was perfect! Soon Fräulein Kutschera would return to the abbey to complete her preparations for becoming a nun, and Mitzi would return to school. Everything would be normal again.

5

GUITAR-PLAYING GOVERNESS

October 1926

"HOW DO YOU DO, CAPTAIN!" the voice boomed through the hall.

Georg sat up straight, startled out of the Saturday newspaper that he always enjoyed just after lunch. He had been engrossed in an article about the growth of a new movement in Germany: Hitler Youth. Georg hadn't been paying much attention to the German news lately, but something had long disturbed him about the arrogant leader of its Nazi Party, Adolf Hitler. This new organization seemed to be all about turning mere children into party members. Very irregular, he grumbled to himself. Austria would never allow such a thing.

Georg realized with a chuckle that the woman with the unusually loud voice at the front door had mistaken Hans the butler for himself. He leaned forward in his easy chair to catch a glimpse of her through the doorway of the sitting room, but Hans blocked his view.

"The captain is within," said Hans in his haughtiest voice. "May I tell him who is calling?"

"I have come to report for duty, sir," replied the woman cheerfully. "I am Maria Kutschera." She paused, as if expecting recognition, and then added, "From Nonnberg Abbey. For . . . for Maria von Trapp."

Hans nodded. "Follow me, Fräulein," he said, and stood back to allow the visitor inside. Quickly, Georg sat back so that he wouldn't be caught peeking. In another moment Hans entered the room and said, "Maria Kutschera from Nonnberg Abbey to see you, Captain. May I show her in?"

"Of course, Hans," said Georg, standing up. Hans stepped aside, and suddenly Georg found himself facing a sturdy, tall, pleasant-faced young woman. On her head rested an odd leather hat that reminded him of a fireman's helmet, and she wore an ugly brown dress, the likes of which he hadn't seen on a woman in at least ten years. In one hand she held a guitar case, and in the other she held a worn brown satchel.

Georg couldn't help staring at the young woman, her appearance was so unusual. Hans cleared his throat and prompted him, "Will that be all, Captain?"

"Oh . . . yes, Hans. Thank you," said Georg. Recovering his manners, he smiled at the woman. "Fräulein Kutschera, welcome to the Villa Trapp. I did not expect you so soon! I am Captain von Trapp." He extended his hand, and they shook.

"Good day, Captain von Trapp," replied Maria. "How do you do?"

"Very well, thank you," said Georg. "Will you sit down?" He gestured to the sofa.

Maria obliged, and Georg returned to his own chair just as an elderly woman entered the room from another door. She stopped suddenly when she noticed Maria. "My apologies, sir. I didn't know you had a visitor."

The woman turned to leave, but Georg called her back. "Baroness, please come meet the newest member of the staff. Fräulein Kutschera, this is our longtime housekeeper, Baroness Mendelsloh. She is in charge of the household, and she also helps the children with their needs."

Maria flew to her feet and gave an awkward curtsy. "How do you do, Baroness Mendelsloh."

Baroness Mendelsloh frowned at Maria. One did not curtsy to a housekeeper. Really! "How do you do,

Fräulein?" she said coldly. She gave Georg a quizzical look and waited.

"Baroness," Georg said to her, as Maria sat down again, "I did not have the chance to tell you, it all happened so fast—just yesterday, in fact. Fräulein Kutschera is here to be Mitzi's governess for the remainder of the school year—Dr. Wagner's orders because of her heart murmur, as you'll recall. Her name is Maria, too, so we will have to remember to call our Maria by her nickname, Mitzi."

Baroness Mendelsloh's eyes widened, and she nodded gravely. "Oh, I see."

"She is a postulant at Nonnberg Abbey," Georg continued, "and she'll be returning there next summer. Fräulein Kutschera, where do you come from? Before the abbey, that is."

"I was born in the Tyrol, and many of my mother's relatives live there still, but I grew up in Vienna," answered Maria. "My father died when I was young, so I lived with relatives until I went to teachers college."

"Ah, Vienna!" said Georg approvingly. "I have some happy memories of that beautiful city. Did you enjoy the coffeehouses and museums while you lived there? They were such delights to me during my visits."

"On occasion I visited coffeehouses with my friends, but I didn't have much opportunity to visit museums. I did attend as many concerts as I could. I love music almost more than eating."

"Ah," said Georg with a serious nod, "that I can

understand. Music is one of my great passions, too. In fact, the whole family loves music; I hope you will feel right at home here." He stood up. "Let me help you with your things, so that you can get settled in your room. Do you have any other luggage coming?"

Maria stood and shook her head. "No, this carpet-bag is all I have, and it isn't heavy at all."

Georg's eyes widened in amazement. "That's all?"

Maria chuckled. "They don't allow us possessions at the abbey, you know. We must give up everything we own when we arrive, so I had very little to bring."

"Ah, understandable, of course," said Georg. "We must help you add to your wardrobe a little while you're here."

"Thank you, Captain. And please, call me by my nickname, Gustl," said Maria with a broad smile at both Georg and Baroness Mendelsloh, who stood waiting for his next instructions. "Fräulein Kutschera is so . . . stuffy."

Georg nodded, but the housekeeper lifted her chin indignantly. "And you may call *me* Baroness Matilda," she said. Clearly, she didn't like this newcomer's rather obvious hint that the baroness was "stuffy" for be-ing called by her title. "The children should call you Fräulein Kutschera or perhaps Fräulein Maria."

Maria seemed not to hear her. Instead her face bright-ened as if a light bulb had turned on. "The children!" she cried, turning to Georg. "May I meet them?" As much as she did not want to leave the abbey, she dearly loved children and missed her students at the abbey school. She had been looking forward to meeting the seven motherless von Trapps and especially little Mitzi.

"Of course," he said, and went to the bottom step of the long staircase in the hall. Maria and Baroness Matilda followed him. Craning his head upward, Georg yelled, "Children, come here, please! Everyone!"

Not a sound could be heard from the second floor, so he finally took out his boatswain's whistle. "Cover your ears," he told Maria. The baroness already had hers covered. Hans, who stood near the door, simply closed his eyes to brace himself. Then Georg blew the piercing signal that called all the children at once. It reverberated through the house, causing a piercing pain to shoot through Maria's head.

"I usually signal them this way only outside," he told Maria. "They must have their doors closed right now."

Maria nodded, secretly thankful to hear this news. She didn't think she could bear hearing that shriek often. Suddenly, a pounding overhead seemed to shake the house as an army of little feet thundered across the ceiling.

"Coming, Papa!" called several voices.

In a few moments, seven children of various sizes dressed in blue sailor suits marched down the stairs two by two with a tall boy leading. Seven pairs of eyes quickly surrounded Maria, gazing at her with curiosity. Suddenly, she felt like a museum display. She took a step back self-consciously, clearing her throat and pasting a friendly smile on her face. Her confidence had vanished.

Georg moved next to Maria. "Children, this is Fräulein Kutschera."

"Call me Gustl," interjected Maria nervously. "Please. It's short for Augusta, my middle name."

Baroness Mendelsloh cleared her throat in disapproval but said nothing.

Georg continued. "Fräulein Kut—I mean Gustl will be staying with us until the end of the school year. She'll be Mitzi's governess, so that she can stay home as Dr. Wagner ordered without having to repeat her grade."

"Hello," said all the children solemnly.

Maria couldn't help but notice that the girls were studying her clothes, which made her even more uncomfortable. She knew the dress and hat were dreadfully ugly, but the mistress of novices hadn't given her a choice. The dress was the only one that had fit her athletic frame.

To cover her discomfort, she put down her guitar and satchel and clapped her hands. "Now which one is my namesake?" asked Maria, scanning their faces. "Hmm, let me see if I can guess."

Quickly, her eyes alighted on Mitzi, whose shy smile and bright pink cheeks gave her away. "It must be you!" she cried triumphantly, pointing at Maria.

Maria nodded with a giggle. "But everyone calls me Mitzi."

"It is so wonderful to meet you, Mitzi," said Maria with a warm smile. She squeezed her new student's hand. "I'm sure we'll have a lot of fun together." She turned to look at each of the children. "It's wonderful to meet all of you!"

"Why don't you show Gustl to her room, Mitzi—the corner room on the third floor?" suggested Georg. He turned to Werner and gestured to Maria's satchel and guitar. "Werner, you follow behind them with Maria's things, will you? And Maria—I mean, Gustl—I hope you will join us for dinner this evening, when we'll all get acquainted. I'll introduce you to the children properly then."

"I look forward to it, Captain von Trapp," said Maria politely, and then she followed Werner and little Mitzi up the stairs to her new room.

~

Maria sat on her bed, gazing at her room in both awe and increasing anxiety. Never in her life had she had such an enormous bedroom. Was this how all the servants lived—with a hand-carved four-poster bed, a mahogany dresser, and fine art on the walls? She wondered if she could return to the abbey after living so many months in such luxury.

Still, she was so homesick already that she choked back a sob. She knew that the doctor had ordered this time away from the abbey so that she might heal from her constant headaches, but she wished she had had some choice, some say in the matter—or at least some warning! Only this morning Reverend Mother had called her into her office and surprised her with a simple question: "What is the most important thing in life?"

Relieved that she wasn't in trouble for a change, Maria had immediately answered with confidence, "The most important thing in life is to find out what is the will of God and then to go and do it."

"Even if it is hard?"

After considering for a moment, she had shrugged her shoulders. Life was hard sometimes. She knew this from experience and had accepted it long ago. "Of course, even if it is hard."

Reverend Mother had then leaned back in her chair and observed Maria soberly for a moment. Then she explained the call that had come for a temporary governess for a local aristocratic family. Maria had been chosen for the task.

"Send me away?" Maria had cried in dismay. "Oh no, Reverend Mother, I want to stay here. I don't want to go away!"

"Even if it is the will of God?"

Maria was silent.

"Baron von Trapp was a captain in the Austrian

Navy, one of the great heroes of our nation. In fact, he was awarded the highest honor the navy can bestow, the Maria Theresian Cross, which also made him a baron," Reverend Mother continued.

"Captain?" repeated Maria in horror. A haughty, aristocratic baron she could manage, but how could she serve a stern, grim-faced naval captain? She had never even seen the ocean!

Reverend Mother assured her that he was known to be a kind man and that the job would last only for ten months, after which Maria could return to the convent to continue her postulancy.

And Maria could only agree, even as tears welled in her eyes. If this was God's will, then to the Villa Trapp she must go. Conflicting emotions of dread and hopefulness had battled within her as she boarded the bus to Aigen and made her way across the city. When she saw the grand house at last, her tears started to flow again, but underneath them a part of her looked forward to meeting the children.

Taking a deep breath, she wiped her eyes and gathered her courage as she made her way up the driveway. Perhaps being a governess would be a fun diversion before she said good-bye to the outside world forever, she told herself. It would be a way to take one last look at normal life before returning to her secluded existence within the abbey. With this thought, she had straightened up, marched to the front door, and rung the bell.

Now, though, as she sat on this strange bed in this

luxurious room, Maria felt lost, as if she had entered a different world. Another wave of homesickness overwhelmed her, and she bowed her head with her eyes squeezed tight. In her imagination she pictured her small, plain cell in the convent with her simple bed and the crucifix hanging on the wall over it. She pictured the sisters and the chapel where they spent so many hours in prayer. Maria had always loved adventures, but she felt at home in the convent. She felt at peace. She felt secure.

This new adventure was God's will, she reminded herself. Opening her eyes, she took a deep breath. When God called someone to a difficult task, she reminded herself, He always provided the necessary help.

6

VISIT FROM A PRINCESS

A week later

WHAT ABOUT THIS ONE, GUSTL?" asked Hedwig, pointing to one of the patterns laid out on the bed. "I think this one is stylish, but it looks comfortable, too—just right for a governess."

Maria picked up the pattern and scrutinized the drawing of the dress on the front. Agathe and Mitzi, who lounged comfortably on the bed with Hedwig, peered at the pattern, too.

Agathe nodded. "Yes, Gustl, pick this—"

A little giggle rippled through the room. Agathe snapped her head up just in time to see two little heads disappear from view. Maria's bedroom door slammed shut with a bang.

Agathe scowled. "Johanna and Martina—that's the third time now." She raised her voice and called, "Stop bothering us!"

Maria smiled, more amused than annoyed. "What do they want?"

"Oh Gustl," Mitzi said, shaking her head. "They always like to sneak around and spy on people. They're just being pests."

"*I'm* too old for silly games like that," said Hedwig with a sniff, and a toss of her glossy bobbed hair.

Maria smiled and squeezed Hedwig's shoulders. "Yes, you are getting to be quite a young lady at nine years old, aren't you?" Then she moved toward the door. "But maybe Martina and Johanna would like to join us. We don't want them to feel left out, do we?"

Hedwig shrugged her shoulders. "I wouldn't mind," she said unsympathetically. "Like Agathe said, they're pests."

Maria laughed but opened her bedroom door a crack to peek into the hallway. "Ah, I thought you'd be standing there," she said, and opened the door wider. "What are you two sillies doing?"

"Scaring you!" shouted Martina, bounding into the room with her hands held out like monster claws. Johanna followed her, throwing a triumphant grin at her annoyed older sisters.

"Well, maybe you should help me pick out a pattern for my new dress along with your sisters," suggested Maria. "Would you like that?"

Johanna grabbed Maria's hands and tugged on them impatiently. "Can you read us a story instead?"

Maria hesitated. She had been spending most of her time with her young student this first week and seeing the rest of the family at meals. In the evenings she had been staying in her room to give the family some privacy. "Won't your father be expecting you downstairs in a few minutes? I thought he liked to read you a story at night. It's almost eight o'clock."

"He doesn't read to us much. We all sing together instead, after he gives us music lessons. He's teaching Rupert and Werner right now. We have time for a story. Please? I even brought a book, see?" She held up a large picture book of *Snow White and the Seven Dwarfs*.

"We're looking at patterns," said Mitzi with a huff. "Go away. Papa is going to call for us soon."

Maria picked up Martina and placed her free hand on Johanna's shoulders. "Oh, we have time for a story. Mitzi, we'll decide on the pattern after they go to bed, all right? Come, let's sit on the carpet by the fire."

Johanna and Martina followed Maria to the hearth, where a fire crackled cheerfully in the darkening room.

Johanna sat down next to her and snuggled close, while Martina plopped heavily onto her lap. "Oof!" grunted Maria. "My, you are a big girl. Comfortable?"

The little girls nodded contentedly, while the older ones grabbed pillows and curled up on the bed to listen.

Maria had nearly reached the part where Snow White ate the wicked queen's poisoned apple, when someone knocked lightly on the door.

"Come in!" chorused the girls.

The door opened to reveal the housekeeper. "Good evening. Your father is asking for you girls in the sitting room. I believe he is ready for your evening musical practice."

"Thank you, Baroness Matilda," said Maria. "I'll send them down in just a moment." The housekeeper bowed slightly and shut the door. Maria chuckled. "What a mercy your papa didn't call you with that whistle! You'd better go now. We'll finish the story soon."

The big girls groaned and pulled themselves lazily off Maria's bed. "I don't feel like singing tonight," said Agathe with a yawn.

"Me neither," agreed Hedwig.

Martina got up with a sigh of regret, for Snow White was her favorite story. Johanna twisted herself around to face Maria. Wrapping her arms around Maria's neck, she laid her cheek against Maria's and sighed happily.

"I like the way you read stories, Gustl. Will you read to us every night?"

"She's here to teach me school," retorted Mitzi as she straightened her dress and smoothed her hair, "not to read stories to you."

Johanna only hugged Maria tighter and closed her eyes. "She doesn't teach you *all* the time. She has time at night, like right now." She leaned back and gave Maria a loud kiss on the lips. Martina slipped her arms around Maria's waist from behind and hugged her gently. "You're nice, Gustl. You're better than all our other governesses," she said shyly.

For a moment Maria sat petrified with fear, for she could not remember ever having been kissed in her entire life. She had seldom even been hugged. It just wasn't done in her family, and only occasionally had her friends hugged her. But as the warmth of the little girls' affection flooded through her heart, she began to relax. Tears came to her eyes as she opened her arms wide to both Johanna and Martina and hugged them tight. "Oh, you wonderful, sweet girls. Of course, I will read you stories often. It would make me very happy. But now you had better do what your papa says."

"Why don't you join us, Gustl?" suggested Agathe as she opened the door.

"Yes, Gustl," agreed Hedwig as Mitzi nodded. "Come sing with us."

"We saw your guitar," explained Agathe. "You could help me accompany our singing. Can you sing, too?"

Maria wasn't sure what to say. After all, she was only a governess. "Uh . . . yes, I love to sing and I do play the guitar, but it's your special family evening. I wouldn't want to impose. I'm sure your papa would rather spend time with just you."

"But Papa suggested it himself," Hedwig reminded her. "At dinner the night you came he said you should join us sometime. Don't you remember?"

"I thought he was just being polite," said Maria.

"Papa never says things he doesn't mean," said Agathe. "Please come. We do it most nights anyway, so it's not a special evening. And it's fun! You should hear us. We're quite good!"

Mitzi smacked Agathe lightly on the arm. "Humble, too. My goodness, Agathe!"

Agathe stood her ground. "Well, we are! Gustl might have fun listening and singing with us instead of just sitting up here all by herself." She turned back to Maria. "Will you come?"

Maria stood up and smoothed her dress. "Well, just for a while, then. If your father seems annoyed at all, I'll say good night. Thank you so much for the invitation."

Hedwig marched to the corner where Maria's guitar stood ready like a sentinel and picked it up. "Come on, Gustl!"

Maria had always loved games and singing and ad-

ventures, but she couldn't remember having more fun
than she did that night. Georg welcomed her warmly,
putting her at ease, and then he had each of the children perform. They either played a piece on their instruments or sang a song, and then everyone taught her
one of the family's favorite songs, a silly song about a
sheep. Then Maria played and sang one of her favorite
folk songs from her childhood in Vienna. After that,
Georg led them in song after song until Martina began
rubbing her eyes. Except for the naval folk songs that
Georg had taught the children, Maria knew most of
the music, so she was able to accompany the family on
her guitar along with Agathe.

Nothing was the same after that night. Maria had always liked the children she taught at the abbey school,
but she experienced a new kind of joy with the von
Trapp children. She quickly came to love all of them.
She guided Mitzi through her studies and enjoyed every
minute of it. When the school day ended, she looked
forward to seeing the rest of the children. They in turn
eagerly shared with her all their daily adventures and
struggles. In the evenings she either read to the little
ones and then spent time privately in prayer or she
joined the family in their musical evenings.

Maria soon learned, too, that all the children enjoyed
games and outings as she did, but most of the time they
stayed indoors at home. Though Georg was kind and
loving, he was still a sea captain at heart and kept the
household to a strict routine out of habit. Even when

he was gone on one of his frequent, mysterious trips, the days marched on with the regularity of a clock.

The children didn't mind their routine, for it seemed normal to them, but to Maria it was far too dull. With Georg's permission she began planning little week-end adventures for all the children except Mitzi, who had to stay quiet in the house. They enjoyed rambles through the countryside, hikes in the nearby mountains, and picnics in the last heat of autumn. Sometimes she would teach them new games, such as volleyball, and she never ran out of stories or new songs to teach them.

With his gentle smile, Georg stepped aside and watched from a distance whenever he was home, which soon became more often. He was not a man for excitement apart from battle. He enjoyed traveling, camping, and hunting on occasion, but when he was home, he preferred music, political discussions with his friends, good books, and his pipe. To see his children enjoying games and outings with Maria gave him deep pleasure, and as the weeks and months passed, he even found himself joining in on occasion.

He needed the exercise, he told himself, but soon he realized he enjoyed being in Maria's presence, even when she sat quietly mending the children's many stockings. She would hum in a chair by the fire after the children had gone to bed, darning the holes as quickly as she could (for she hated the chore) while he smoked his pipe and read his book. They didn't speak much, but Georg found himself comfortable and content. She wasn't his beloved Agathe, of course, but somehow Maria seemed to belong there next to him. He couldn't quite imagine her returning to the abbey next summer. Deep down he began to dread her departure.

Spring 1927 seemed to sneak up on the von Trapp household. Maria had kept the children so busy that none of them had noticed the time passing. Now it was late March. The snow was melting, and the trees and flowers were once again nodding hello to the world. With them came new games and outings with Maria, and Mitzi was finally strong enough to join them sometimes.

That spring also brought a special visitor.

"Tante Yvonne!" cried Johanna one day as she glanced out the nursery window after hearing a car door slam. "Hedwig, look, it's Tante Yvonne!"

Maria looked up from the arithmetic textbook she had been studying to plan tomorrow's lesson. For several months now, she had been not only Maria's governess but also the younger girls' nanny and teacher. The last nanny had flounced away in a huff when Martina decided that she wouldn't cooperate with anyone but Gustl "because she likes us and smells much better."

"Who is Tante Yvonne?" asked Maria.

"Our mother's cousin," replied Johanna. She waved frantically, her nose pressed to the glass. "Hello, Tante Yvonne! Hello! Up here!"

"She doesn't see us," said Martina. "Come on!"

Johanna and Martina raced out the door and clattered down the hall.

"Quietly, quietly!" came the stern voice of Baroness Mendelsloh. "You are turning into a pair of hoodlums!"

Maria winced, feeling a pang of guilt. The housekeeper had indicated more than once that the children had become rambunctious ever since she had arrived. This was a quiet, sedate home, Maria reminded herself. She must learn to be calmer and more ladylike so that she could be a better example to the children.

Hedwig had paused on her way out the door to peer into the mirror and tidy her hair ribbon. She turned to Maria. "Aren't you coming, Gustl?" she said. "Tante Yvonne is a princess, and you must greet her down in the hall along with the other servants."

Maria's heart flew into her throat. "A princess? Are you sure, Hedwig? A real princess?"

Hedwig giggled and grabbed Maria's hand to pull her to her feet. "Of course she's a real princess! She's also a countess. She lives in Vienna, and Papa has been planning to marry her; but with you here, I don't think he wants her anymore. Come on!"

Following Hedwig down the stairs and hoping her

hair still looked neat, Maria considered her strange comment. Why would Georg no longer marry the princess just because the children had Maria as a governess? There was no time to think about that now, though. She, a common young woman, was about to meet a real live princess!

As she and Hedwig approached the hall, Baroness Mendelsloh stood at the door to the drawing room, beckoning them. "Hurry, hurry!" she hissed. "Princess Yvonne is walking up the steps now."

Maria and Hedwig slipped into the drawing room to join the rest of the servants and children, who stood in a stiff line ready to receive the princess. Everyone but Martina, who seemed confused about all the fuss, had a nervous expression on his face.

In another moment Georg entered the drawing room with a petite, dignified-looking lady on his arm. "Tante Yvonne is here, everyone!" he announced with a broad smile, as if none of them had any idea she was coming.

The servants and children swept into either bows or curtsies, the children adding "Hello, Tante Yvonne" or "How do you do, Tante Yvonne?" Maria nearly pitched forward onto her face, for she had never learned how to curtsy properly. Red-faced with embarrassment, she managed to straighten along with everyone else, and no one seemed to have noticed her awkwardness.

Maria studied the princess carefully as she said hello

to each of the children and nodded pleasantly to the servants. Fairy-tale enchantress she was not with her perfectly coiffed, chestnut-brown bob and her thin eyebrows that marched across her forehead in a nearly straight line. But she was handsome and regal looking, clearly at ease with her station in life. Yes, she would be perfect for Georg, and the children would need a new mother after Maria returned to the abbey.

"Yvonne, may I introduce the newest member of my staff, Fräulein Kutschera?"

Maria, lost in her scrutiny, nearly jumped when she heard her name. Now she realized that Georg was leading the princess to her. Stretching out her hand to shake Maria's, Princess Yvonne smiled, her eyes cool but not unfriendly. "Well, well," she said, "here is the wonder girl I have heard so much about. It's a pleasure to meet you, my dear."

Maria smiled and replied, "It's a great honor to meet you, Princess. Please, call me Maria." She wondered if she had addressed the princess correctly and what, exactly, Princess Yvonne had heard about her. As the princess and Georg left the room, Maria let out the breath she had been holding. Thank goodness that was over, she thought. Still, how exciting to meet a real, live princess!

For the rest of the afternoon school was put aside, so that the children could visit with their aunt. Maria gladly stayed in her room to plan for tomorrow's lessons. Meeting the princess was exciting but a little overwhelming. Again, she noted how different the world of the von Trapps was from the world she had always known. She longed for the simple life at Nonnberg Abbey and the dear nuns. Only a couple more months . . .

Suddenly there came a sharp knock on her door.

"Come in," called Maria, looking up from her books.

When the door opened, Maria's eyes widened with surprise. "Princess Yvonne!" she cried, jumping up from her chair. As she did so, she banged her leg hard against the desk and yelped.

"My dear, are you all right?" asked the princess with an expression of genuine concern.

Maria hobbled over to the princess with a strained smile, trying not to rub her sore spot. "Oh yes, yes, I'll be fine. Please, sit down." She gestured to her wingback chair in the corner.

"Thank you," said Princess Yvonne, delicately perching on the edge of the chair. Maria sat in the opposite chair and waited expectantly.

For a moment the two women gazed at each other curiously. Maria couldn't imagine why royalty would want to visit with her, but she didn't know how to ask. Then the princess spoke in a cautious tone.

"My dear, I really must talk to you."

Maria was silent, too baffled to encourage the princess to continue.

Princess Yvonne cleared her throat. Then she asked, as calmly as if she were asking the dinner menu, "Do you realize the captain is in love with you?"

Maria jumped up as if bitten by a snake. "What? But . . . but Princess, that's—"

"True," supplied Princess Yvonne matter-of-factly. "It's perfectly true. Oh, I don't think it will last long, of course. You are too young and energetic for him. I'm certain that he is merely infatuated. I just wanted to tell you so that you might stay away from him a little more and not be such a distraction to him. After all, he is planning to marry me."

Maria sank down in her chair, so distressed she could hardly think. "Of course, of course. I didn't know. I will leave for the abbey this afternoon."

Startled, the princess shook her head. "No, no, Fräulein Maria, that is not what I was suggesting. And you have certainly done nothing wrong."

"I must," insisted Maria, wringing her hands. She squeezed her eyes shut and wondered how this could have happened. "Will you kindly look for another teacher for Mitzi?"

"But why?" cried Princess Yvonne. "This is no reason to run away. The captain and I have already straightened things out, and he is not truly in love—just a little bit. It is because you are so good with the children. Perhaps a little too wild with them, but that is all right. I will straighten that out later."

Maria opened her eyes and looked imploringly at Princess Yvonne. "But how can I act natural, knowing this now?"

"Why, just act as you always have before. We will be engaged soon, I am sure. Then on the day of the wedding, which will likely be in the summer, you will throw a little party for the children while we are at the church. Afterward you may return to the abbey and your life as a nun."

Maria wrinkled her brow in confusion. "Won't they be at the wedding, too?"

Princess Yvonne laughed at the thought. "Of course not! Just think what a commotion that would be— seven children at a grand, formal wedding!"

Maria frowned, suddenly irritated with the princess. If she didn't want the children to celebrate such an important occasion as that, then why did she want to be their second mother?

"The honeymoon will last several weeks, of course," continued Princess Yvonne. "When we return, it will be time for school. Georg and I have agreed that the children's manners are suffering lately, so we will put the girls in the Sacre Coeur boarding school and the boys in the Jesuit College. There they will get to know other youth of their social status and become the ladies and gentlemen they must be someday. If you stay until the wedding, everything will work out splendidly!"

Maria's heart sank. Boarding school? She knew it

wasn't polite or ladylike to question the princess, but she couldn't help herself. "Why do you want to marry the captain, then, if you want to send the children away?"

Princess Yvonne's eyebrows shot up, as she surveyed Maria with curiosity. "Well, my goodness, did you think I was marrying the children, my dear? What a strange young thing you are!"

Maria had heard enough. It didn't matter that the princess considered her a "strange young thing"; she couldn't stand the idea of the household being upset in this way. "It doesn't matter," she said stiffly. "I cannot stay any longer. I will pack my bags today."

Standing up, Maria grabbed her satchel from the closet and began pulling clothes out of her dresser. Princess Yvonne, now quite nervous, followed Maria and placed a hand on her arm. "Please, Fräulein Maria, please don't leave. I didn't mean to upset you so."

Maria shook her head and continued emptying her drawers. "I must. It wouldn't be right for me to stay, knowing the captain has feelings for me. It's time for me to go home."

Princess Yvonne stood for a moment in silence, her hands clasped tightly together. Then she turned sharply and left the room. Only then could Maria breathe freely again.

Late that afternoon, Maria finished packing, grading assignments, and writing notes for the children's next governess. After casting a final, regretful glance around her room, she crept downstairs with her satchel and guitar in hand. As she turned the bend in the staircase, she paused. She didn't want Georg to know she was leaving, but she couldn't face walking out the door without saying good-bye to the children. How could she, when she loved them all so much?

For several minutes she stood in an agony of indecision. Finally, she decided that slipping out without being noticed was the only way to avoid uncomfortable questions from Georg. Besides, if she saw any of the children, she might not be able to leave.

She was just tiptoeing to the front door when a voice broke the silence.

"Fräulein Maria?"

Hans. She might have known he would notice her. Maria grimaced but turned around with a bright smile on her face, as if she were merely going out for a stroll.

The butler looked at her coat and luggage and seemed uncertain of what to say for a moment, but at last he merely said, "Fräulein, I was just coming to tell you that Princess Yvonne is asking to see you in the library."

Maria didn't know what to do. Hans would mind his own business, she knew, but would the princess? Clearing her throat nervously, she asked, "Uh . . . just the princess?"

Hans studied her, his brow furrowed. "No, Fräulein, the princess and Father Gregory. I believe the captain is playing on the back lawn with the children." He stretched his lips in the semblance of a smile. "Practicing his volleyball serve, it appears."

This was good news. Maria was happy to see him spending more time with the children instead of traveling so much. Reluctantly removing her coat and hat, she laid them on her luggage and followed Hans to the library.

Seated on comfortable chairs with a reading lamp between them, Princess Yvonne and an elderly priest with a long gray beard waited expectantly. Maria paused in the doorway, reluctant to go in. What could a strange priest want with her?

Princess Yvonne and the priest stood up. With a smile the princess gestured to the priest and said, "Fräulein Maria, this is my confessor, Father Gregory."

Hans shut the door, and Maria faced the princess and the priest alone. This was surely one of the most uncomfortable moments of her life. And what if Georg returned to the house and found her luggage in the hall? She prayed the conversation would be over soon.

"Good day, Father Gregory," Maria greeted him, with as warm a smile as she could muster. She posed her face in a look of relaxed friendliness.

Princess Yvonne gestured to a third chair nearby, and the three of them sat down.

"Fräulein Maria," she began, "I have not shared our little conversation earlier today with Georg. I am hoping that it won't be necessary. That's why Father Gregory is here."

Maria was both relieved and confused. "Oh?"

Father Gregory leaned forward and smiled kindly at Maria. "You must understand, my child, that Georg's affection for you is nothing serious. We think that you are just so popular with his children that he can't help but feel something more than friendliness for you. At the same time, if you leave now, there is a real danger of kindling this affection into something . . . well, deeper —into the kind of romantic affection that neither you nor Princess Yvonne want."

Maria stared at him in consternation. What kind of puzzlement was this? Were all men so contrary?

"Therefore," Father Gregory went on earnestly, "I counsel you to do what the princess asks and—"

Dropping her head into her hands in frustration, Maria interrupted him. "Father, I cannot do that. I just can't."

"But my dear child, this is God's will," Father Gregory pointed out, as if anyone could see that. "God would not want you to do anything to interfere with the captain's marriage."

Maria straightened, closed her eyes, and sighed.

"You see, Father," pointed out Princess Yvonne in a tone of satisfaction, "I told you she was a sensible girl."

Father Gregory took Maria's hand and placed his other hand on top of it. Then he waited until Maria opened her eyes and met his gaze. "Now, promise me that you will stay here until Captain von Trapp and

Princess Yvonne have been married. Will you do that?''

Swallowing hard, Maria replied flatly, ''I promise I will stay—but only until June 30, because then I will be received into the Benedictine Abbey of Nonnberg. That has been the arrangement since I arrived.''

With a gentle squeeze of her hand, the kind old priest said, ''All right, my child, go in peace now.''

But as Maria trudged up the stairs and began putting away her clothes, she felt only anxiety about the three months remaining before she could return home. All she could do now, she decided, was to try to avoid the captain as much as she could and pray that he became engaged very soon.

7

CLOSED DOOR, OPENED WINDOW

May 1927

THE LATE-SPRING AFTERNOON SEEMED to sparkle with romance as Georg and Princess Yvonne strolled through the garden. Everywhere on her lush estate, trees and bushes were in full blossom, and the lake beyond the garden sparkled in sheer delight as the sunlight cast its warm rays over the world.

Georg tapped the small box that lay in hiding at the

bottom of his pants pocket. Yes, this would be the perfect setting, he decided. There was no reason for delay any longer. He had received his answer from Maria simply by watching her avert her eyes and sidle around him whenever they encountered each other. He had no idea what he had done to offend her, but it was clear that she didn't think much of him. It was time to focus on the princess and let go of the young woman who had captured his children's hearts.

"What a lovely arbor," he commented to distract himself. He stopped to gaze at the latticed structure to the side of the path.

Princess Yvonne smiled. "Yes, in the summer it is simply covered with beautiful pink roses. Sometimes I come here just to be surrounded by the fragrance. It's heavenly."

Georg gestured to the small bench inside. "Why don't we sit for a moment?"

For a few minutes they sat in silence, enjoying the fresh spring air. Georg searched for the words to make a proper proposal and had just decided how to begin when a deep voice broke the silence. "Ahem."

Georg and Princess Yvonne looked up to see Charles, the palace butler, standing at the entrance to the arbor. Holding a small silver tray in his white-gloved hand, he said, "Pardon me, Captain von Trapp, but this just came for you from Aigen. It's registered, so I thought it might be important."

"Yes, thank you, Charles," Georg said with a smile,

accepting the small envelope that lay on the tray. With a crisp click of his heels, Charles turned and disappeared.

"This is from home," said Georg, ripping the seal. "I hope everything is all right. Excuse me for a moment, Yvonne."

As the princess waited politely, Georg read the letter. Then he reread it, for it made no sense. The notecard was in Fräulein Maria's handwriting, but it had no greeting or signature. All it said was, "My eyes are none of your business. I thought you were a man who kept your word. I am sorry, I was mistaken."

Georg read it yet again, uncomprehending. Then, all of a sudden, he remembered the note he had sent to her a few days earlier. In one part of it he had written, "I wish I could see your eyes when you read the announcement of my engagement."

Slipping the notecard into his vest pocket, he stood up and walked a few steps away from Princess Yvonne. He stared toward the distant mountains and rubbed his mustache thoughtfully. Part of him was angry with Maria for taking offense at his comment, for he had meant nothing inappropriate by it. But another emotion, deeper within his heart, was rising to the surface, and soon he understood what it was. The truth, he realized, was that he loved Maria—for herself, not just for her relationship with his children. He loved the temperamental, brash young woman who wore them all out with picnics and hikes and lawn games every week. How curious, he mused. She was nothing like his calm, gentle Agathe, God rest her soul, and even less like elegant, dignified Yvonne. But somehow she had his heart, and it was time for him to face it.

"Well, what's the matter?" asked Princess Yvonne. "Is anybody ill?"

Georg whipped around, startled out of his reverie. "No, no one is ill." He patted his vest pocket as if seeking inspiration from the notecard inside for what to say next. Then he walked back to the bench and sat down with his hands out. Yvonne took them and looked at him expectantly. As he paused, he could see the dawning awareness in her eyes that he would not be making a proposal.

"The truth is, Yvonne," he said slowly, "I know now that I cannot marry you. When I proposed to you three years ago, I was ready, but you let me wait too long and now I have changed. The truth is . . ." He cleared his throat awkwardly. "I love somebody else now."

Princess Yvonne gently withdrew her hands and bowed her head. For a few moments she was silent; then she nodded. "Thank you for telling me, Georg. It's all right."

"Can we remain friends?"

Smiling graciously, she gave his hand a squeeze. "Of course. I have known you so long, Georg, that I can't imagine you as no longer part of my life."

"I appreciate that. Perhaps, though, it would be best

if I returned home now," he suggested. Standing up, he offered his arm to the princess, and they returned to the palace in sober silence.

~

Maria cautiously climbed the tall ladder that Hans had set up for her. Above her head the hall chandelier shimmered as if to say it didn't want a bath today, thank you very much. Below her Hans lifted some soft cloths and a small bucket of cleaning solution onto a ledge attached to the ladder. Maria dreaded the chore, but all the maids were busy with their spring cleaning tasks, and both Hans and Baroness Matilda had their hands full with running the household as usual. With grim determination she positioned herself where she could reach the chandelier and began to wash the crystal drops.

She wiped her sweaty brow in the June heat. If only they had begun weeks ago, when it was cooler! Still, she shouldn't complain. She would have to clean the chandelier only once, for in twelve more days she would return to Nonnberg Abbey, never to leave again.

Suddenly, Johanna, Martina, and Hedwig hurtled past her to Georg's study down the hall.

"Watch it!" cried Maria, gripping the ladder in terror. "You'll knock me over if you're not careful."

"Sorry, Gustl!" Hedwig yelled back as she knocked on the study door.

Maria shook her head and returned to her task. What were they up to? she wondered. Then she scoffed to herself. Well, how else were they supposed to see their father? He had been locked in his study almost every day since returning from Princess Yvonne's estate, even during meals. When Maria did see him, he seemed preoccupied and unhappy, and he hardly spoke to her. Was a happily engaged man supposed to act like that? Or maybe he had been hurt by her angry note and wanted nothing to do with her anymore. She couldn't blame him. How she wished she hadn't written that! She felt awful now, but she had no opportunity to make an apology. Oh, when would she learn to control her temper?

At that moment the three girls came dashing back again, this time stopping at a careful distance from the ladder. "Papa says he doesn't know if you like him at all! Do you?" demanded Johanna, while Martina and Hedwig watched her with stern expressions.

Maria was struggling with a crystal nearly out of her reach, so without pausing she answered absentmindedly, "Of course I like him. What a silly question!"

Without a word the girls disappeared again, and Maria immediately forgot the conversation as she reached for another crystal drop. Never in her life had a cleaning task been so tedious! She pitied the maid whose job it would be next time.

The strain of the heavy cleaning day was forgotten

by evening as Maria added the final touches to a fresh flower arrangement on the hall table. As she trimmed the fragrant, pink peonies and placed them just so in a large oriental vase, a voice cut through the silence.

"That was really nice of you."

The unusually warm, rich tone of Georg's voice caught Maria's attention. Turning to him, she met his eyes and immediately dropped her own in confusion. Something different was in his expression, not just his voice. "Wh-what did I do that was so nice?" she asked cautiously, thinking again of the awful note she had written during his visit to Princess Yvonne's estate.

Georg frowned. "Didn't you send word to me through the children that you accepted my proposal? That you want to marry me, I mean."

Maria's scissors clattered to the floor, along with the rest of the peonies. She stared at Georg, dumbfounded. "That I want to . . . marry you?"

Shifting nervously, Georg thrust his hands in his pockets. "Well, yes. The children talked together this morning and then came to me with the suggestion that the only way to keep you with us—for we all want you to stay—is for me to marry you . . . so that you could be their second mother. I told them that I would like to but didn't think you liked me much, so they went and asked you and said you told them yes. I thought . . . I thought that meant you agreed to marry me."

Maria floundered for words. This was the last thing she had expected! What had happened to the princess?

"But . . . Georg, you know that I am about to return to the abbey. I cannot marry anyone and also be a nun."

Sadness filled Georg's eyes. "Is this your last word?" he asked mournfully. "Is there absolutely no hope?"

Filled with conflicting emotions, Maria hesitated. She liked Georg very much, and she loved the children, but she had committed herself to becoming a bride of Christ long ago. How could she turn her back on Him as her bridegroom, when she had promised Him? But now an idea came to her. "Well," Maria replied slowly, "I can ask the mistress of novices. Whatever she says I consider to be the will of God, for it is my duty to obey her. I'll go see her tomorrow, all right?"

Removing her apron and forgetting all about the mess on the floor, Maria hurried away without waiting for Georg to respond. Surely, the mistress of novices would tell her that fulfilling her commitment to be a nun was a higher calling than accepting Georg's marriage proposal, she told herself. Once she satisfied him with the nun's answer, everything would go back to normal.

The next day she arrived at Nonnberg Abbey, anxious for the unpleasant errand to be over as soon as possible. Thankfully, she had to wait only a short while for the mistress of novices to arrive in the parlor.

"Maria!" she cried with a smile. "What are you doing here in the middle of the week? I didn't expect to see you until your usual Sunday visit."

Maria poured out the whole story of Georg's proposal and her desire to know God's will. "I know I should certainly say no, of course," she finished, "but I told him I would hear the answer from you, just to be sure."

The mistress of novices considered Maria's words solemnly for a moment; then, without a word, she stood and left the room. Perplexed but determined to see her task through, Maria sat quietly for a very long time. What was happening? Surely, the nun wasn't ignoring her, but even conferring with Reverend Mother wouldn't take this long.

Finally, when Maria felt as if she couldn't wait another minute, the mistress of novices returned and said, "Reverend Mother is waiting to see you now, Maria. Come with me."

Eagerly, Maria followed her through the cloister and up a flight of stone stairs to Reverend Mother's office. If the decision came directly from her, Georg would certainly feel at peace about Maria's refusal to marry him.

The mistress of novices allowed Maria inside and then left the room, closing the door behind her. With a broad smile, Reverend Mother stood from behind her enormous desk and came around it to greet Maria.

"How wonderful to see you, my child!" she said.

"Hello, Reverend Mother," Maria replied, kneeling and kissing her ring. "How have you been?"

"Very well lately," the kind old nun replied, gesturing for Maria to sit down. "My arthritis has not acted up for several weeks now, thanks be to God." Turning the chair next to Maria's so that it faced her, she sat down. "And how are you?"

Maria blushed and shook her head. "Oh, Reverend Mother," she said with a deep sigh. "Everything seemed so clear to me for so long, but now I am so confused."

"The mistress of novices has explained to me what happened," said Reverend Mother gently, "and because it is such an important moment in your life, the entire community assembled to pray and discuss it. We want to help you understand God's will. It has become clear to all of us"—she paused and took Maria's hands in hers before continuing—"that it is the will of God that you marry Captain von Trapp, that you accept his proposal and be a good mother to his children."

Maria stared at Reverend Mother without understanding. Words stood out to her, but they made no sense—*will, accept, good mother*. What did they mean? Gradually, they sorted themselves out in her mind, and she realized that Reverend Mother was telling her not to return home to the abbey in a few weeks but instead to marry the captain.

A storm of emotions arose in Maria. This can't be right, she thought. How could God simply reject her like this? Why wouldn't He want her to dedicate her life to Him as a faithful nun who spent her days in prayer? She opened her mouth to argue and then snapped it shut. It was no use, she knew. Reverend Mother's instructions were always final. There could be no arguing, no questioning. At Nonnberg Abbey, that was never allowed. Maria closed her eyes, trying to force herself to accept Reverend Mother's pronouncement as God's will.

Her throat dry and her heart full of rebellion, Maria looked down at the nun's ring. The words that encircled its amethyst said, "God's Will Hath No Why." She swallowed and blinked back tears. When God expressed His will, a faithful Catholic was supposed to obey, not demand an explanation. But why was it so hard? She didn't want to obey, and she did want God to explain Himself! Then she looked up at the face of Reverend Mother, where tears of compassion filled her eyes. Her lips moved soundlessly in prayer, as if she understood that there were no words to make this moment easier for Maria.

At that, all the rebellion in Maria's heart ebbed away, like floodwaters after a storm. She had given her whole life—her whole heart—to God, but He had never promised to fulfill her every wish or to make obedience easy. Following Him meant giving Him everything, even her wishes and desires.

Tears flowed down her cheeks as Maria asked humbly, "What does God want of me now, Reverend Mother? I feel lost and adrift. My whole life is shifting beneath my feet, and I don't . . . I don't know how to bear it. Please help me."

Reverend Mother squeezed her hands encouragingly. "God wants you to serve Him well where He needs

you most—and cheerfully with joy in your heart. Can
you do that?"

Sobbing now, Maria nodded. "I will try, Reverend
Mother. I know He will help me."

Reverend Mother placed her hand gently on Maria's
cheek and smiled into her eyes. "Go in peace, my child.
All will be well. You must trust Him."

Unable to stop crying, Maria could only nod and
hold Reverend Mother's hands tightly for comfort. Finally, she gave a shuddering sigh and said, "I will try
to trust Him, Reverend Mother, I promise. Thank you
for your guidance. I'll go back now and tell him yes."

On November 26, 1927, Maria returned once more
to her cell in the abbey, where her three fellow pos-
tulants dressed her in a delicate silk bridal gown and
lace veil. When she was ready, the mistress of novices
crowned her with a wreath of sweet, white edelweiss
and kissed her cheeks. Then, for the last time, Maria
walked through the ancient abbey where she had spent
two happy years. All the sisters lined up for their
farewell, watching Maria approach the heavy oaken
doors that separated the nuns from the world beyond.

As they slowly opened, Maria knelt before Reverend
Mother for her final blessing. Then, her eyes misty with
tears, she rose and took her place for the processional.
Ahead of her to the soft strains of Bach, she could
see Agathe and Mitzi lead Georg down the aisle to the
front of the church. He was resplendent in his navy
dress uniform—truly a handsome man, Maria realized

for the first time. Behind her, Hedwig, Johanna, and Martina carefully smoothed her long train.

When the majestic sounds of the pipe organ began, it was time to enter the packed church. Then, with Rupert and Werner accompanying her on either side and the little ones following in their beautiful white dresses, Maria took her first step toward Georg and into her new life as Baroness Maria von Trapp.

8

A CHANGE OF DESTINY

September 1932

"Oh, I am so glad to be home," said Maria with a heavy sigh as she and Georg slowly climbed the front steps, "and I have missed the children so much, especially the babies. Do you think Lorli and Rosmarie have truly been all right with the nanny? They are so little yet."

Lorli was only a year old, and Rosmarie was three.

"Of course they are all right. Fräulein Kofler has been satisfactory in every way so far, and all the children seem to like her."

"I suppose," Maria agreed, sounding as if she didn't suppose at all. "It was a beautiful vacation, though, wasn't it, Georg? I wish I hadn't needed hospitalization for those kidney stones, of course, but the stay in Veruda afterward was just what I needed to feel like myself again."

Georg nodded. "I agree, my dear; I feel like a new man myself. And we had hardly any rain this time. Hello, Hans!"

The butler held the door open for them with a warm smile. "Good afternoon, Captain and Baroness. It's wonderful to have you home again."

"It's good to see you," Georg replied. He gave his hat to Hans, who hung it on the hat stand. "Has everything gone well? Any special news?"

"The last few weeks have been very warm," answered Hans, "but the house has been run as smoothly as ever, Captain. Frau Resi did take to her bed for a few days with a cold, but Baroness Matilda was quite skillful in the kitchen, and all is back to normal now."

"Glad to hear it, glad to hear it."

"I am looking forward to Resi's dinner tonight," said Maria. "I wrote to her and asked her for her *Wiener Schnitzel* our first night home. I have been longing for it for weeks! I hope she hasn't forgotten."

Hans nodded. "The kitchen does smell delicious

right now," he said. "And I think she is preparing a special dessert in your honor as well. It's a—"

Maria held up a hand to stop him as she climbed the first step to the second floor. "No, no!" she said. "I want it to be a surprise. Every dessert she makes is wonderful. I can hardly choose a favorite. Georg, let's go see the children. The luggage can wait."

Georg and Maria had almost reached the top step when the hall telephone rang. They stopped and waited for Hans to answer it. Telephone calls were usually important. In another moment Hans came to the bottom step and called, "Captain, it's long distance from Zell am See."

Georg and Maria looked at each other in dismay. Long distance! Austrians seldom made a long-distance call unless it was an emergency, for such an extravagance was expensive. Georg quickly descended the stairs. Maria followed more slowly, feeling as if her stomach were turning inside out. She clutched the banister, willing herself not to fall or be sick. Whoever the caller was, she knew, would almost certainly have bad news.

Georg took the receiver from Hans and cleared his throat as Maria sank into a nearby chair and fixed her eyes on the telephone. "Hello? This is Georg von Trapp."

As Georg listened to the caller, his eyes grew wide, and his body seemed to freeze. Maria's anxiety grew.

Something was seriously wrong. When he leaned his head against the wall and squeezed his eyes shut, Maria stood up and drew near him.

"I see," he said to the caller at last. "That is very bad news, to be sure. I hardly know what to say, except to thank you for telling me personally." The calmness of his voice soothed Maria's nerves a little but not for long. "It's all right," Georg said to the caller after a moment. "Please give my regards to Mrs. Lammer. I know how hard she tried to save the bank. Good day, Mr. Koch."

Georg placed the receiver onto its cradle and stood quietly a moment, chewing his mustache and blinking rapidly. Maria realized that he was trying to keep tears from flowing down his cheeks. Tentatively, she placed a hand on his shoulder. "Georg? Save the bank? What's happened?"

Georg sighed deeply, keeping his eyes focused on the wall. Maria waited patiently for him to compose himself. Finally, he turned to look at her, his eyes full of despair. "That was Mr. Koch from Lammer and Company Bank. Our bank. You know that since Hitler cut off all tourist trade to Austria—to force us to surrender to the Third Reich—our bank along with many others have been struggling to survive."

Maria nodded.

"They had already been under strain since the financial collapse . . ."

Maria grabbed Georg's arm.

"And yesterday, the Lammer bank went bankrupt. All its customers lost their money, including me."

Maria said nothing, stunned into silence.

"Our money is gone, Maria," explained Georg. "All of it. We have a little stashed away here in the house, but . . ."

"I don't understand," said Maria. "When Mrs. Lammer told you the bank was struggling, you pulled all the money from your London bank and deposited it with Lammer to help. It was so much! How could it not be enough?"

"I do not know," he said with a helpless shrug. "Hitler's reach is just growing too powerful. Lammer isn't the only one. Several banks have closed." Georg dropped his head in his hands, stricken with shock as the implications of the disaster sharpened in his mind. "Maria, we have nothing. Nothing! How could I withdraw all the money from London? Why didn't I leave some there?"

"Georg, you didn't do it carelessly. You did it to help a friend in a desperate situation. That's what the Gospels tell us to do, remember? Whatever we do for the love of our Lord Jesus Christ, He will reward a hundredfold—and on top of that, He gives us eternal life. You took a risk, but it was for a noble, honorable reason. I am proud to be your wife. I truly am." Wrapping her arms around him, she hugged him tightly. "It will be all right, I promise. I grew up with very little money. It is only a return to normal for me."

Georg leaned his head against hers and let the tears fall. "But the children, Maria. The poor children. How will we provide for them? We have quite a bit of real estate, but we can't sell that if we want to secure their futures. What can we do?"

Maria was quiet, thinking. Strangely, she felt calm and even a little cheerful. She did not feel especially grieved to learn the terrible news—not for herself, anyway. Money never had much appeal for her, but for Georg, she understood, money meant a life of comfort and privilege, the only kind of life he had ever known.

"I don't know the answers, Georg," she finally said. "I don't know what we'll do. But all is not lost. I know it isn't. God loves us and will never leave us. Not for a moment."

∼

"Our money is gone! Our money is gone!" Hedwig, Johanna, Martina, and Rosmarie danced in a circle hand in hand in the sitting room as the rest of the family watched with a mixture of amusement and consternation. In the middle of the circle, baby Eleonore, nicknamed Lorli, squealed in delight and clapped her hands.

Werner, now sixteen years old, shook his head in mild exasperation. "I don't think they understand."

"No, they don't," agreed Maria. "But that's all right. The important thing is that the rest of you do." Sitting back against the sofa, she looked at Georg, who sat next to her. He seemed relaxed, one leg crossed over the other, one arm resting against the back of the sofa, but she could tell he didn't feel relaxed, for he was chewing on his mustache again, a telltale sign.

"What will we do, Papa?" asked Agathe from her seat on the floor. "Girls, stop that noise, will you?" she said to her giggling sisters. "We're trying to have an important conversation."

The little girls ignored her until Georg said, "Yes, girls, please stop and sit quietly. We need to discuss this as a family, and your ideas might be very important. I wish Rupert were here to discuss this with us."

Maria patted his arm. "I will go to Innsbruck next week and tell him the news. He needs to know right away, since we must stop sending him an allowance."

"I'm afraid we'll need to take away more than that," said Georg. "He will have to work his way through university now if he really wants to become a doctor."

Hedwig plopped down next to Maria on the sofa and snuggled against her. "What do we need to discuss?"

"Well," said Maria, "we must figure out how to manage without much money. All of us must contribute ideas and help. I have a little notebook and pen with me, so let's hear your ideas. I'll write them down."

Everyone sat quietly and tried to think of ideas, except for Lorli, who had stopped squealing and was now trotting around all the sofas and chairs in the sitting room. Being frugal was new to the family, for the von Trapps had never needed to worry about money before. It had simply always been there. Maria glanced at their worried faces, as well as Georg's discouraged one, and said, "Well, I have one idea to get us started. Do you think we could handle all the household chores together?"

Mitzi replied, "Of course, but we have servants to do that."

A look of understanding crossed Werner's and Agathe's faces. "We will need to let go of our servants," Agathe said.

Georg nodded reluctantly. "Yes. Most of them, anyway. Let's talk about that later, though. They might hear us."

"Well, we can do the chores," said Werner. "We're strong. We just need to learn how."

Mitzi and Agathe nodded.

"We could raise chickens, too," said Hedwig. "We had chickens back at Martinschlossl, remember?"

"What about selling the house?" suggested Werner. "We would probably get lots of money—"

"No," said Georg, interrupting with a firm shake of his head. "No, this is our home. Perhaps some of our land in Munich, but most of our properties we will keep in the family for your futures. Other ideas?"

Everyone thought hard. Finally, Werner brightened.

"Papa, I'm almost seventeen now. Why don't I try to find work somewhere?"

Georg thought for a moment. "Perhaps you could find some odd jobs nearby. You may look into that."

"And after I visit Rupert at the university," said Maria, "I will go to Nonnberg Abbey to ask them to pray for us."

"We should all start praying," pointed out practical Johanna, now thirteen years old. "Remember, last night we heard in our Gospel reading that Jesus promised, 'Whatsoever you shall ask, you shall receive.'"

As the days passed and the family gradually adjusted to their new life, they began to pray together for guidance every night before their family hour of singing and games. Discussing ideas for how to save and earn money was easy enough, but it was not so easy for Georg to sell a small piece of his land in Munich or to sell his beloved car or to dismiss all his faithful servants, except for Hans the butler and Resi the cook. Nor was it easy to face his friends, who soon learned of his bankruptcy and seemed worried that he would beg them for money. And although twenty-year-old Rupert took the news about his allowance with a cheerful smile, it wasn't easy for Maria to tell him he must bear the burden of paying for medical school alone.

Gradually, the family learned how to clean and to care for the animals and gardens and to take the bus or bicycle wherever they needed to go. The children found the chores more amusing than dreary, so everyone did his fair share, even three-year-old Rosmarie, who learned how to feed the chickens and set the table for meals. To save on heating and cleaning, Maria closed the large rooms on the first and second floors of the house, leaving the third floor for the family's sleeping and living quarters.

One day, soon after Maria returned from visiting Rupert at the university in Innsbruck, she took the bus to Nonnberg, as she had promised. The family had made many changes in just a few weeks, but they still needed prayer, for they could do only so much to stretch the money they had left. Also, Georg was depressed, and Maria was worried about him.

Still, she felt light and hopeful as she watched the fields and houses fly past the window during the bus ride. Deep inside, she felt an odd sense of expectancy and anticipation, as if the von Trapps had not experienced a disaster but were instead approaching a new beginning that lay just around the bend. Something was in the air; she could feel it. Besides, returning to tasks she had known before her life as a baroness was both a pleasure and a welcome challenge. She couldn't wait to see the beloved old nuns, anyway. It had been too long.

Reverend Mother immediately agreed to add the von Trapps to their daily prayers, and the mistress of novices had a practical idea. "Why don't you ask Archbishop Ignatius for permission to have a small chapel prepared in one of your rooms? Many castles and estates have one."

"I didn't know that," said Maria, her brow knitting in thought. "But Sister, how will that help us?"

The old nun beamed and spread her arms wide, as if to say the answer was obvious. "Don't you see? If you had a chapel, he might send a priest to stay with you to say daily Mass, which would strengthen you all during these trying times. Plus, it would give you a little extra income, for the priest would pay for his room and board. And then you could rent the other rooms that you are no longer using to students from the Catholic university."

Maria was thrilled by the idea. Even better, the kindly archbishop readily gave his consent, so with the help of the local parish church, the huge dining room was soon prepared and consecrated for use as a chapel. In just a short time, a young priest occupied one of the second-floor rooms. His name was Father Dillersberger, and he was a theological professor who taught at the nearby Catholic University of Salzburg. For him the situation was just right. He had been seeking a quiet place to write a scholarly book. In the morning he said Mass; during the day he studied, wrote, and taught classes; and in the evening he gave Benediction.

Even better, he brought with him two more board-ers, and soon the von Trapps were earning enough money to take care of their needs, though certainly with none to spare. As the months passed, the boarders gradually began to join them in the sitting room in the evening, where the fireplace spread its friendly warmth. Within a year the old villa was full of laughter and fun and spirited discussions as boarders came and went from the nearby university. Of course, the family also continued their evening singing, to the boarders' delight, and by now they had also learned Gregorian chants, Bach chorales, and other sacred music to sing during the Sunday Masses.

Although money was no longer plentiful and Georg continued to struggle with discouragement sometimes, God's blessings were rich and beautiful. Through their struggles the von Trapps had become closer than ever, and Georg and Maria realized with pride what wonderful children they had, for none of them complained or grumbled about the changes in their lives. And because Father Dillersberger said Mass every day, the Holy Eucharist was ever present in their home. How could money compare with something as wonderful as this?

The family might have continued in this manner indefinitely, but one spring day close to Easter, Father Dillersberger made a journey home to visit his ailing father. In his stead, his friend Father Franz Wasner came to take his place and changed the course of the von Trapps' lives forever.

At first, no one suspected anything, for it all started without fanfare. The morning after Father Wasner arrived, Maria invited him to join the family in the kitchen for breakfast near the warm stove. The other boarders had already left for the day. Tall and thin, the priest folded himself awkwardly into a chair and surveyed with pleasure the warm, crusty *Semmerl*, homemade raspberry jam, and fresh butter.

"This smells delicious, Baroness von Trapp," he said. "Did you make the jam yourself?"

Maria chuckled and poured the priest some coffee as the children waited quietly for the breakfast blessing. "No, Father, I've never been much good in the kitchen. Resi, our cook, makes the jams, using recipes passed down from her mother. She makes the rolls fresh every morning, too."

"Will you have some cream with your coffee, Father?" asked Georg, holding up the small pitcher.

"Yes, please," said Father Wasner, and he poured a little cream into his cup. "And now I will bless the food."

Breakfast was lively that morning, for Father Wasner was interested in everyone and had many questions. He wanted to know what Agathe and Werner were doing now that they were graduated from high school, where Rupert was, what the younger girls were learning in their studies, and what games and stories Rosmarie and Lorli liked best.

"You all sing very well together, too," he observed after he had learned a little bit about each family member. "Do you do that often? Sing for each Mass, as you did this morning?"

Georg shook his head. "Not every day, but we do

always sing at our Sunday Masses. Father Dillersberger especially enjoys the Bach chorales. Do you sing, Father?"

The priest nodded. "Yes, I do sing some, but I am more of an instrumentalist. I play piano and organ. As a boy I was formally trained in Vienna."

"You will have to play for us some evening during our family singing hours," suggested Maria.

"We sing together almost every night," explained Johanna. "We have ever since I can remember. And we all play instruments, too."

"If Father Wasner plays something with us, we could have an orchestra!" cried Martina, who was now twelve.

"Well, not quite," said Georg with a smile, "but close!"

"I would enjoy your evening singing very much," said Father Wasner. "I need music like I need air. But I would not want to impose on such a special time for your family."

Georg waved his words away. "Not at all! We often have our boarders join us in the evenings. The more, the merrier. Sometimes, when we sing the old folk songs, it gets quite rowdy!"

"It's a lot of fun," agreed Hedwig. "You can join us tonight."

"When we need to rehearse for the Masses, though, we gather in a smaller room away from everyone," explained Maria. "It all works out splendidly."

Father Wasner nodded. "I see. That's wonderful."

Removing his glasses, he polished them on his shirt and added thoughtfully, "Now this morning, you know, you really sang quite well. Beautifully, in fact. But . . ."

Maria's eyebrows shot upward. "But?"

Father Wasner replaced his glasses and folded his arms across his chest, frowning into space as if puzzling over an idea. "But I think you could do even better."

"How so, Father?" asked Georg.

"Well, in the motet you sang this morning, you made a mistake that, if you could fix it, would make the music absolutely soar."

"Perhaps you could show us, Father," suggested Maria. "We would love it if someone with expertise could help us improve."

Father Wasner buttered a bite of his roll and sipped his coffee. "All right, then, let me hear the motet again, so that I can find the place where I noticed the problem."

"Right now?" asked Georg, his coffee cup halfway to his lips.

"Of course." Swallowing his bite of roll, the priest stood up and made a sweeping motion with his arm. "Everyone."

The well-mannered von Trapps had never sung at the breakfast table before, but this was for a priest, so dutifully they began to sing. Over the next few days, in fact, they could hardly stop singing. Father Wasner was full of energy and ideas. He worked with them through their entire repertoire for Masses, finding all their weak spots and teaching them how to improve.

After Father Dillersberger returned to take back his room, Father Wasner went home to the seminary, but he still came to visit the von Trapps almost every day to work on their music. Throughout the summer they sang as they never had before. They perfected songs they had learned long ago, and they learned new, more complex songs that they could have never handled alone. With Father Wasner's help, it seemed, they could now learn anything. They sang madrigals, ballads, chants, motets, chorales, carols, new folk songs, and anything else that he suggested.

No one but their boarders ever heard them sing, for they sang only for God and for the pure love of music. Yet in this way, without even realizing it, the von Trapp family became artists.

9

A SURPRISE PERFORMANCE

July 1934

HURRY, EVERYONE, Father Wasner will be here in about a half hour," urged Maria, waving impatiently at her family as they drank glasses of lemonade. They had just finished a busy Saturday morning doing chores. "We have to practice."

Martina set her glass on the patio table and wiped

her mouth. "Mother, it's so hot. Can't we go inside to practice?"

"It's too stuffy inside," said Hedwig. "Let's stay out here."

"Why don't we go behind the pine trees on the side of the house the way we did last week?" suggested Georg. "It was quite pleasant back there."

Everyone liked this plan, so they moved to the shady spot and took their positions. Georg made himself comfortable on the park bench set among the trees. The family choir was complete without him. They had two sopranos (Johanna and Agathe), two second sopranos (Mitzi and Martina), two altos (Maria and Hedwig), one tenor (Werner), and one bass (Rupert). Although Georg had a fine voice, he preferred to conduct in Father Wasner's absence and puff his chest with pride. Rosmarie and Lorli liked to watch by his side or play games when they grew restless.

First, Georg led the group in some scales and other exercises to warm up their voices. Then he said, "What shall we work on first, so that we're ready for Father Wasner when he comes?"

"Don't we need to work on the new madrigal, 'The Silver Swan'?" asked Agathe.

Maria nodded. "Yes, Georg, let's do that one. Remember, we were planning to surprise him. He has no idea we've been working on it. Let's practice 'Jesu, Meine Freude' first, though, since we're singing that at Mass in the morning."

"That's a good plan," agreed Georg as he poised himself to conduct. Raising his hand, everyone stilled in anticipation of the first note. He gestured for the family to take a breath; then he brought his hand down, and the family began to sing:

Jesu, meine Freude,
Meines Herzens Weide,
Jesu, meine Zier!

On and on they practiced, until Georg was satisfied with their work. Then he said, "All right, everyone, let's move on to 'The Silver Swan.' Remember the English pronunciations that he taught us, so he is impressed instead of amused."

The silver swan, who living had no note,
When death approached unlocked her silent throat.

Somewhere in the distance a car door slammed, but everyone was too focused on the music to pay much attention. It must be Father Wasner, Maria thought. He would be able to hear them from the driveway. Wouldn't he be surprised!

Leaning her breast against the reedy shore,
Thus sang her first and last, and sang no more,
Farewell all joys, O death come close mine eyes,
More geese than swans now live, more
    fools than wise.

As the last note faded away, the von Trapps were startled out of their reverie by the sound of enthusiastic applause on the other side of the pine trees. Excited, everyone waited for Father Wasner to turn the corner, his face shining with pride. Georg stepped around the trees to greet him, only to surprise everyone by exclaiming, "Frau Lehmann! What an honor this is!"

In the next moment, to everyone's astonishment, Georg returned with a pretty, dark-haired young woman beside him.

"Lotte Lehmann?" gasped Maria, recognizing her instantly.

The young woman laughed and stepped forward to shake Maria's hand. "Yes, that's me! And what an honor it is to meet you all!"

The family stared at the famous opera soprano. They had just heard her on the radio last week! She was even more beautiful than they had imagined.

"Here I come to seek a room to rent," Lotte continued, "and I find a singing family!"

Georg smiled and modestly waved her words away. "Oh, Frau Lehmann, we are just amateurs."

Lotte turned to him with her eyebrows arched. "You are not 'just' anything, Captain von Trapp. I am quite serious. You have gold in your throats!"

The family looked from one to the other with a mixture of pleasure and embarrassment. Maria found her voice. "Oh, Frau Lehmann, Georg and I had the privilege of hearing you sing once in *Der Rosenkavalier*, and it was simply breathtaking. To have you here to visit us is . . ." Maria's words failed her, so she finished with a dramatic wave of her arm.

"Did you say you are here to rent a room?" asked Georg.

"Yes," replied Lotte. "The Salzburg Festival begins tomorrow, you know, and I am here to enjoy the concerts. I had another room reserved at an inn, but unfortunately a pipe just burst there and caused serious flooding and damage to the building, so they had to cancel my reservation."

"Well, we do have an available room," said Maria, "and we would be delighted to let you have it for as long as you like. Agathe here will see you to the room and make you comfortable, and you may settle your payment with our butler, Hans."

With a smile Agathe stepped forward to lead Lotte Lehmann back to the house, but Lotte was not yet finished. "That is wonderful; thank you so much. But oh, your singing! This family must not keep such a precious gift to itself! You must give concerts and share it with others. You must share it with the world— perhaps even go to America!"

Georg smiled and nodded his head in thanks. "Frau Lehmann, you are too kind. We are not performers, though. We sing only for our own pleasure and for the Masses held in our family chapel. Would you like to attend tomorrow morning? Mass begins at nine. We'll be singing 'Jesu, Meine Freude.'"

Lotte turned to Georg and looked him in the eyes.

She placed a hand softly on his arm to focus his attention. Then she said slowly, "Captain von Trapp, I know world-class singing when I hear it. I meant it when I said you have gold in your throats. You could touch the whole world with your music. A singing family! It's unheard of!"

Something inside Georg began to twist in discomfort. He wanted to change the subject, but she clearly had more to say.

"Now, hear me out," she said. "Tomorrow afternoon is the group singing competition at the festival. It is not too late to sign up. Please, you must take part in that contest. You simply must!"

Now everyone was aghast. "Oh, we couldn't, Frau Lehmann," said Maria in dismay. "Truly, we have never sung for the public in our lives—none of us. We aren't ready for something like that. Indeed, I doubt we ever will be!"

The children nodded in emphatic agreement. Perform on a stage? In front of Salzburg? For a competition? Never!

Now Georg was stepping away from the great opera singer, shaking his head slowly but determinedly. His eyes had lost their friendly glint. "Frau Lehmann, truly, we are very honored by your words, but it is simply out of the question."

Maria couldn't help but feel a pang of disappointment. As frightening as the idea was, it also sounded exciting. How fun it would be to share their hard work with the people of Salzburg and possibly win a prize! But she understood. As a baron and an Austrian Navy officer, Georg was right. Such things were simply not done by members of the nobility. To put themselves on public display would be a great embarrassment for the whole family and especially for Georg, who had so recently lost his fortune.

Lotte Lehmann was undeterred. With a twinkle in her eye, she grinned at Georg and then at everyone in the family. "I understand you perfectly," she said. "But I would argue that as patriotic Austrians, you have a duty to share your gift with your fellow countrymen. There is nothing undignified about it, Captain. If it were, do you think I would go on stage myself? I have my pride, too. How about just this once? I would be so very pleased. In fact, I can make the call to enter you in the contest as soon as I settle into my room. What do you say?"

The von Trapps gazed back at her, speechless with uncertainty, excitement, and fear. Finally, Georg nodded reluctantly in consent. "Just this once . . . for Austria."

~

The audience fell silent as Herr Sommer, the director of the group singing competition, took the stage. Every eye fixed on the small envelope he held in his hand. Twelve groups had competed for first prize, each group singing three Austrian folk songs. Now it was time for the award ceremony.

Maria and the children had performed in utter misery, sick with stage fright and confusion. Singing for a few boarders in their family chapel at Mass was nothing like this! The brilliant spotlight, the hundreds of eyes, the rustling programs, and the detached faces of the judges were like nothing they had ever experienced before or even imagined. As they took the stage, Maria had squinted into the light and found Georg in the fifth row. He smiled encouragingly as they sang, but his eyes were pained. Oh, she thought, if only they had never let Lotte Lehmann talk them into this!

But it was over now. In just a few minutes they could go home. Scanning the children's faces next to her in the seats reserved for the competitors, she could see they were anxious for this to be over as well. How good it would be to go home tonight, laugh about their experience over dinner, and return to normal life! Perhaps they would buy a luscious *Linzertorte* at the local bakery to celebrate.

Poor Georg, she thought. Although he hadn't sung with them, she knew that the embarrassment he felt was worse than anything she or the children felt, for such antics as competing in a music festival would bring a judgmental gaze upon him from all his friends and associates. If only Herr Sommer would stop drawing out the anticipation and award the prizes already!

Herr Sommer could not be hurried, though. Slowly, he withdrew the envelope and read the names of those contestants who were awarded the honorable mentions, the third prize, and the second prize. Maria clapped heartily for all of them, but now Herr Sommer was talking about the history of the festival and what an honor it was to host such marvelous musicians and singers every year and how the winners of the contests would join the ranks of many illustrious winners before them, and so on and so forth. Maria was becoming too impatient to sit much longer, and she began bouncing her knee in growing agitation. Craning her neck to her left, she could see Georg sitting a few rows away, chewing on his mustache as he always did when he was distressed. Hold on, Georg, she thought. It's almost over, and we can go home. This will be funny tomorrow, I promise!

"And now, what you have all been waiting for!" announced Herr Sommer grandly. "The first prize of the 1934 Salzburg Festival group singing competition is awarded to . . . the von Trapp family of Aigen!"

Maria burst into applause for the lucky winners. Good for them! she thought magnanimously. Now, which ones were they? All the contestants had performed beautifully, but she couldn't quite place the. . .

"Baroness von Trapp!" hissed an usher. "It's you they are calling. You need to go to the stage."

The children were standing, wide-eyed and disbelieving, waiting for Maria to get up and lead them out of their row.

"Me?" gasped Maria, her eyes swinging back to the stage where Herr Sommer smilingly beckoned to her. "It's . . . oh, my goodness!" Quickly, she shot upward and hurried toward the stage. The usher stood aside as the family filed out of their seats and followed her.

The next five minutes were a blur of thunderous applause, Herr Sommer's enthusiastic congratulations, much hand shaking, and an award certificate, which was thrust into Maria's hands. With a pang, Maria realized that Georg's seat was now empty, clearly because their victory only increased his embarrassment. Would he ever recover from this? Awkwardly, the von Trapps smiled and bowed to the audience and to Herr Sommer one more time before finally returning to their seats. Their adventure was over at last.

It appeared to be, anyway. The summer's excitements soon faded, and August's heat changed to the crisp chill of autumn. Soon the younger children were back in school, and snow returned to Salzburg. As Christmas approached, the Villa Trapp took on several new boarders. With the extra money, Georg and Maria were able to decorate the house and give the children a few small gifts, as well as a small fir tree that glowed with real candles on Christmas Eve. The memories of the family's victorious moment at the festival were buried under the joys of the season, but no one missed the stage. It was good to return to the calm, steady hum of everyday life.

One day in early January, Hans answered the front hall telephone while Georg was shoveling the front walk outside. "Baroness, it's the radio station in Salzburg," he said to Maria, who was cleaning the dining room nearby with Agathe.

Wiping her hands on her apron, Maria took the receiver from Hans with a quizzical expression. Hans merely shrugged, so she said, "Hello? This is Baroness von Trapp."

"Yes, Baroness, this is Herr Mayr. I am the manager of the radio station here in Salzburg."

"What can I do for you, Herr Mayr?"

"I attended the Salzburg Festival a few months ago and heard your family in the group singing competition. Congratulations on winning first prize! That is quite an honor."

"Yes, thank you, it certainly is," agreed Maria, wondering where this conversation could possibly be going. "If you would like to speak with my husband, I can call him—"

"No, no, there's no need for that," said Herr Mayr. "I am calling to tell you that I would like the von Trapp family to sing on our Saturday evening program."

"Oh!" said Maria. "Well . . . Herr Mayr, we are truly very honored, but—"

"Please be up at the Mönchsberg next Saturday at four. Thank you, Baroness von Trapp."

"But—" began Maria, and stopped. The line had been disconnected. For a moment she stared at the receiver, and then she looked up at Hans, who stood at the front desk, updating the guest registers. "He hung up on me," she said in amazement. "He didn't even wait to hear my answer."

"What was the question, Baroness?" asked Hans.

"It wasn't even a question," said Maria. "He just told me we had to sing on the Saturday evening radio program."

"Oh dear," said Hans dryly, "the captain will not like that."

"No, Hans, he certainly won't," agreed Maria. "I don't even know how to tell him."

"A meal is probably the best time to tell a man anything," suggested Hans. "When his stomach is full."

~

"You said no, didn't you?" cried Georg, wiping his mouth and setting down his fork.

Maria shrugged. "He gave me no time, Georg," she said. "He just told me what he wanted and when to be there, and then he hung up without waiting for my answer. I'll call him right after lunch."

"But Mother," said Hedwig, "perhaps it's God's will for us to sing on the radio."

Maria caught the glint in her eye. Hedwig was only teasing Georg. Still, what if she was right? The fact that the family did not want to perform again in public did not necessarily reflect God's will. Perhaps He wanted them to perform, no matter how they felt. After all, even for Georg there was no indignity in singing over the radio, where no one could see them, and their music might bring joy and blessings to many people all over Austria. Could this unexpected opportunity be God's will? The family waited in silence for Georg's decision.

Finally, Georg sighed heavily and bowed his head in defeat. "I can't say I like it, but I do think this is God's will," he admitted reluctantly. "It should be our delight, as well as our duty, to do His will, so practice hard this week with Father Wasner and do your best next Saturday. I will be listening with pride."

The radio program performance was a success, and so were several more later that year, and then life finally returned to normal again—for a while, anyway.

One day in November, a letter arrived in the mail from the secretary of Kurt von Schuschnigg, chancellor of the Austrian Republic. Georg read it at dinner with great solemnity as the family listened in astonishment.

"Recently, Chancellor von Schuschnigg had the privilege of hearing the von Trapps' rendition of Bach's 'Hymn of Thanksgiving' over the radio," wrote the secretary. "Your performance was so delightful that he is requesting the honor of another performance at an upcoming reception at Belvedere Palace, which he will

be hosting for a number of national and foreign digni-
taries, as well as the Austrian diplomatic corps and military authorities. You will be one of several featured
performers and will be accompanied by the Vienna
Philharmonic Orchestra in an encore performance of
'Hymn of Thanksgiving,' as well as three other songs
of your choice in the same musical tradition. The reception will be held on Saturday evening, December
21, 1935, at seven o'clock. Please reply at your earliest
convenience."

Georg looked up at his amazed family and then
turned pleadingly to Maria. "That doesn't mean we
must accept, does it?"

Having grown up as a common citizen, Maria knew
far less about aristocratic protocol than Georg did, but
something told her that there was only one answer to
this question. She wanted to reassure Georg that they
didn't have to accept the invitation, but out of her
mouth came "I don't know" instead. It was the gen-
tlest way, really, to tell him that yes, they could certainly not say no. How could they turn down a performance for the chancellor of Austria and so many
important government people? Wouldn't it be an honor
to perform for Austria's officials, rather than an embarrassment or a bother?

Round and round the family went, discussing the
dilemma. Everyone was nervous about the idea of
performing at such an important function—with the
Vienna Philharmonic Orchestra, no less—when they

were still such unseasoned performers. The idea of turning down such an invitation, though, seemed not a dignified choice but an unpatriotic one. This thought was unbearable, for the love of Austria flowed through everyone's hearts. Finally, in the end, the decision was made. Once more—just once—they would sing for Austria. And then, surely, if any more invitations came, the requests would not be so important and could respectfully be turned down.

Yet at the end of the state reception, as Maria and the children sipped punch and basked in the relief that their performance had been well received, the von Trapps' world changed yet again. A tall, cordial gentleman approached Georg and Father Wasner, and before they knew it an entire concert was scheduled for February in the famous Vienna theater called the Musikverein.

"I don't know how it happened," said Georg later to Maria, a guilty expression on his face. "One minute I was shaking my head and politely saying no, and the next I was nodding my head and shaking his hand."

Happen it did, though, and now the relaxed family evenings of singing became focused, serious rehearsals. Father Wasner came as often as he could to direct them, using his musical genius to correct every flaw and to elevate their art ever higher. Never had they worked so hard! Despite their reluctance to continue performing, they all understood that with an entire concert ahead, they must behave like professional singers.

Georg still struggled deeply with the idea of his family performing in public, but bills had been mounting, and he could not deny that the family badly needed the money that the concert would bring. If this were not God's will, he reasoned, He would close the door. In the meantime, he would continue to pray for guidance and trust that he was leading the family where God pointed.

~

The Musikverein is a historic building that houses three auditoriums—large, medium, and small. Being not yet widely known, the von Trapps were assigned the small auditorium, and the great American contralto Marian Anderson was given the large one. None of them minded that most patrons were flowing into the large auditorium; it was quite enough to be performing at all! Even so, their performance was not overlooked, as newspaper reviewers wandered into the small auditorium during Miss Anderson's intermission and discovered what one of them called "the lovely miracle of the von Trapp Family."

He was not the only one to write a glowing review. Within a week, Georg had bought a scrapbook for all the newspaper clippings, and he had agreed to allow the family to perform several more concerts that winter, as well as one at the 1937 Salzburg Festival. Even he had to admit that this was a special honor, since most musicians had to wait patiently for several years before they could perform an entire concert at the festival. With only one singing family anywhere, the von Trapps shot to the top of the list for the very next summer!

Yet, even after Lotte Lehmann herself burst into applause after the festival concert and talent scouts swarmed the family backstage with offers for even more concerts throughout Europe, the von Trapps only smiled and tucked the unsigned contracts safely into their scrapbook. They had had enough excitement. Besides, they had their boarding house to run! As wonderful as the past season had been, it was time to return to ordinary life with its gentle rhythms of school and work.

Little did the von Trapps know, as they returned home to Aigen after the festival concert and put their scrapbook away, that they had only just begun to sing. The very next day, Hans answered the door to a formidable-looking woman with a long red feather in her alpine hat.

"Good day; how may I help you?" he asked in the cold, formal tone he reserved for unknown visitors.

"Good day," said the woman. "My name is Madame Octave Homberg. I am the concert manager for the Homberg and Bellon Musicians Agency in Paris. Is Captain von Trapp or Baroness von Trapp taking visitors at the moment?" She handed Hans her business card, which he took with a dignified nod.

"One moment, Madame," he said, opening the door wider to allow her inside. "Please wait here in the vestibule."

"Thank you so much," said Madame Homberg, stepping inside.

In a few moments Hans returned. "Please follow me, Madame Homberg. Captain and Baroness von Trapp will see you in the library."

Half an hour passed before Madame Homberg sailed from the house with a satisfied expression on her face, leaving Georg and Maria in their library, wondering what had just happened. A signed contract promising concerts in Paris, France, lay between them on the desk.

That was not all! Only three hours later, two more contracts lay on top of the first one—a signed agreement with a concert management agency in Belgium and an unsigned offer to perform in Holland, Denmark, Sweden, and Norway. By dinnertime, they even had a solicitation from a New York City concert manager named Charles Wagner for a second whole season in America!

"An American tour is too overwhelming to consider right now, and besides, that season would start in the fall of 1938—next year," said Georg to Maria and the children that evening as they gathered by the fireplace. "We did not have to sign it right away, so we will discuss it as a family. However, Mother and I did promise the concerts for France and Belgium because they fall within your Christmas break from school. But before we sign this third contract, we thought we should consult you. There are several challenges we must discuss, as well as your feelings on the matter."

"What kind of challenges, Papa?" asked Hedwig, now grown up at twenty. "I think we all agree that we enjoy singing, and we do need the income."

Georg nodded. "Yes, that's true, but . . ." He paused, considering Hedwig's words.

"Well, there is the matter of your studies," said Maria. "Rupert still has medical school to finish in Innsbruck, and Werner has his agricultural courses in Salzburg. Lorli and Rosmarie are too young to go and aren't singing with us anyway."

"Yet!" said seven-year-old Lorli with a hard look at Maria.

With a chuckle she added, "Yet—of course. But Martina is still in high school and would need to come, and we have the boarders here. Performing these concerts would mean taking a few weeks off, and we want to know what you think about that. Would it even be possible?"

"But think of the education we would all receive just by traveling to these countries!" cried Mitzi. "None of us except Papa has ever been outside Austria, and there are so many wonderful churches and museums and historical places to see."

"That's true," agreed Rupert, who at twenty-six was anxious to explore the world before settling down to be a doctor. "I've always wanted to travel around Europe. And really, Papa, there's a good chance that I could take some time off school, as long as I know the dates."

"I think I could, too," said Werner, now twenty-one. "And I'll bet the girls' school would understand and help them keep up with their studies as we traveled."

"What about Father Wasner?" asked Mitzi, who was nearly twenty-three. "We couldn't go without him, could we, Mother?"

Maria sighed. "Oh dear, I'd forgotten about him. Yes, Georg, he's teaching at the seminary and editing a newspaper. How would he possibly find time to get away? I don't see how these concerts are possible."

Everyone was silent, thinking of all the complications.

"Well," Georg finally said, "if this is God's will, He will surely clear our path. I will talk to Father Wasner and see what he says."

To the family's surprise, one obstacle after the other fell away. Rupert, Werner, and Martina were allowed the necessary weeks away from their studies, Father Wasner was able to find substitutes for his responsibilities, and friends agreed to care for Lorli and Rosmarie as well as help Hans and Resi care for the house. Soon, no more obstacles remained, and in November 1937, the von Trapps' first European concert season began.

The fall and winter months flew by in a whirlwind of excitement, music, and enthusiastic reviews. In each country—France, England, Belgium, Holland, and Italy—the family explored the treasures it had to offer between their concerts. They visited great museums and churches, relished food and scenery, and honored historical landmarks. They even walked in the footsteps of some great saints—Saint Francis in Assisi, and Saints Peter and Paul in Rome.

The best part of all was sharing their love of music with others, for all people could speak its language, no matter their nationality. The von Trapps sang for everyone, young and old. They even sang for royalty and clergy, including Pope Pius XI. By the time they returned home in early 1938, they had become rising stars throughout Europe, filled with happy memories of their season abroad and longing for some rest.

It was a hope not meant to be.

SHADOW OVER AUSTRIA

March 1938

"RUPERT, WILL YOU PLEASE TURN ON THE RADIO?" Georg said from his favorite library armchair as the family and Father Wasner—now a cherished friend —gathered to celebrate Agathe on the eve of her twenty-fifth birthday. "I believe they are going to play a symphony by Schubert in a few minutes."

Rupert, who sat next to the radio, obliged with a

167

flick of a knob. Instead of the smooth voice of the radio announcer or the strains of an orchestra, the deep voice of Chancellor Schuschnigg spoke in an urgent tone. "I am yielding to force, for I can do nothing else. If we fight, it will be a bloodbath for our people, for our army is far smaller than that of the Germans. My Austria . . . my people . . ." The chancellor's voice broke, as if he was fighting back tears. He paused for a moment before continuing with as much warmth and conviction as he could. "My Austria, God bless you!"

The von Trapps glanced at each other in confusion as the strains of the national anthem flowed through the room.

"What is going on?" asked Hedwig, turning to Georg. If anyone would understand, he would. Before he could answer, the door opened and in came Hans. He stood straight and dignified, as he always did, but his pale complexion and conflicted expression betrayed a battle of emotions within.

"Captain . . . Baroness," he said haltingly. Everyone turned to him, hoping he had news.

Georg frowned and raised his hand in a helpless gesture. "Hans, do you know what to make of what we just heard on the radio? We turned it on only at the end."

Hans nodded, but his eyes dropped to the floor. "Yes, sir, I do. That's what I have come to speak with you about."

Everyone waited as the national anthem came to its closing strains. Hans cleared his throat. "The German Army has invaded Austria as of just a few minutes ago. The military operation is called the Anschluss—Hitler is joining Austria to Germany. I am here to inform you that I am a member of the Nazi Party, and . . . I have been for some time now. I thought you should know."

The family was horrified at this confession. Their butler? They had a traitor living in their midst!

In the brief silence following the anthem, everyone tried to make sense of what was happening. Then a harsh voice shouted through the radio, "Austria is dead! Long live the Third Reich!" A rousing Prussian military march followed this bone-chilling announcement. Georg switched off the radio and turned back to Hans, who cleared his throat and nervously continued. "I have been loyal to this family for many years, and I am still committed to serving you with that same loyalty as long as you are willing to trust me. I will never betray you. But I understand if you cannot give me your trust." With that, he turned on his heels and strode from the room.

Georg, stunned, locked eyes questioningly with Maria, who had no answers. Across the room Agathe and Mitzi started to cry, and looks of panic were growing on the faces of Hedwig, Johanna, and Martina. Werner and Rupert slumped with their heads in their hands. The little ones scanned the faces of the others for clues to what this was all about, for none of it made sense to them. Then Georg stood up. "Let's all go to the chapel and spend some time in prayer."

The chapel brought little comfort, for through the large, thick-paned windows came the peal of distant bells. Werner opened the window so that they could hear better, and they realized that the bells weren't from only one church but were from many—the cathedral, Nonnberg Abbey, Saint Peter's, the Franciscan monastery, and even more from farther away. Louder and more insistent they became, until the noise was deafening. Werner shut the window, and Maria pulled all the drapes to drown out the clanging. What had once been beautiful and uplifting was now ugly and frightening.

The family returned to the library, unable to pray anymore. Father Wasner eyed the phone on Georg's desk for a moment and then picked it up to call the priest of a nearby parish to see if he could learn more. When he hung up, his expression was pained. "The Nazis are marching into Salzburg right now," he said. "The bells ring for them—to celebrate the invasion. The Gestapo, Hitler's secret police, have a man stationed in every church to make sure the bells ring until they are ordered to stop."

"That's a sacrilege!" cried Hedwig angrily. "How can they do something like that!"

Father Wasner shook his head, too overcome with emotion to say more.

Georg switched the radio back on. "Hear how the whole world greets its liberators with joy!" boomed a triumphant voice. "The people of Salzburg rush to their steeples and ring out the good news for all to hear!"

Werner could not bear the lies. He leaped from his chair with his fists clenched, his face twisted in fury. Georg raised a calming hand. "Anger will accomplish nothing, son," he said. "It will eat us alive if we let it."

"We can't let this happen!" cried Werner, turning upon his father with his eyes blazing. "This is *our* country, *our* homeland! Hitler can't just come in and take it from us and expect us to do nothing! He cares nothing for Austria! He wants only power and glory!"

"I understand," said Georg. "If Austria had any hope of mounting a successful resistance, I would rush out the door to join the fight without a moment's hesitation. But we cannot beat the Germans through the use of force. Our army is far smaller than Hitler's. And we are neither armed enough nor prepared enough to fight back. Right now, prayer is our best weapon. We must entrust the fate of Austria to God, and maybe He will show us what more we can do when it's time."

The lies of the Nazis continued for days afterward, trumpeting the German victory through the radio as the people of Salzburg mourned and tried to adapt to being ruled by the Third Reich. Georg tried to keep his family from going into town, hoping to protect them from the changes happening all over the city as much as possible, but he could not keep the children from school.

One day, Rosmarie and Lorli burst through the door with their eyes wide with amazement.

"Mother, everyone in Salzburg must say 'Heil, Hitler!' now, with one arm stretched out like this." Lorli paused to demonstrate, her right arm pointing stiffly away from her body. "And soldiers are everywhere! They're on every street corner holding big guns."

"And a lot of the street names are different now, and the whole city is like a lake of red!" added Rosmarie dramatically.

"Every house and every store has a big red flag with a black swastika hanging from it," explained Lorli. "You should see it! Are we going to hang one, too?"

Maria flinched as if slapped. "Absolutely not! Never!"

Nearby stood Hans, working on an account book for their boarders. Georg had decided to trust him because he had always been good to them, even when his salary had been cut after their bankruptcy—but Maria was wary. As soon as the words left her mouth, she threw him a worried glance. She could see that he had stiffened, though he had not paused in his work. How long could he be loyal to them? she wondered. Didn't he have an obligation to support the party in whatever ways he could?

Hans wasn't Maria and Georg's only concern. No longer could they trust friends, acquaintances, or shop-keepers, for some of them had become Nazis and might report the von Trapps to the authorities for their quiet resistance to the Anschluss.

Georg showed good cheer and optimism whenever he encountered one of the children, but at night, in the privacy of their bedroom, he poured out his worries to Maria. As much as he loved his homeland, the Austrian government was now in the hands of the Nazis. At any moment they could force him to serve in the navy of the Third Reich. Maria told herself that an Austrian naval captain would be of no use to the Nazis because Austria was a landlocked country, but deep down she worried. The ambitions of Hitler might possibly have no bounds.

After two months of the family keeping peacefully to themselves in Aigen, a long, shiny black car rolled slowly up the driveway and stopped close to where Maria and Georg were weeding the front garden. A tall man in a Gestapo uniform stepped out of the car and approached them with long, stiff strides.

"Heil Hitler!" he cried, shooting his right arm straight in front of him in salute. He waited a beat for Maria and Georg to return the salute, but seeing their hands full of dirt and garden tools, he continued. "Captain and Baroness von Trapp, I come in the name of our great Führer to deliver some important news."

Georg and Maria pulled off their garden gloves and stepped toward the man to greet him politely. Georg smiled and shook his hand. "What is this news?" he asked.

"Our Führer will be paying a visit to Salzburg shortly, and it is my duty to make sure that every house greets him with the flag of the Third Reich." He paused to survey the house. "I can see that you are not yet displaying a flag, and I have been told that you do not own one. Is that true?"

Maria wondered grimly if Hans had at last reported them. Georg only nodded. "That is correct."

"May I ask why?"

Georg's smile widened into what Maria recognized as his mischievous look, and she willed him to behave himself. After all, this was the Gestapo! Terrible rumors had been flying around town that the Gestapo sent anyone they didn't like to filthy labor camps. There the prisoners worked at back-breaking physical tasks and were slowly starved to death. But Georg seemed not to notice her piercing look and cheerfully replied, "Well, you see, one of those grand flags is quite expensive. I simply can't afford it!" Georg shrugged and tried to look apologetic.

The Gestapo officer smiled in a way that reminded Maria of a snake. "One moment, Captain." He strode back to the car and reached inside, pulling out a thick red cloth square. Presenting it to Georg, he said, "There you are, Captain, compliments of the Führer. You will put it up right now, won't you?"

"Oh, I don't think so," said Georg smoothly, tucking the flag under his arm. "Thank you so much, though."

The officer's face darkened. "And why not? I will help you if you need it."

Georg shrugged again, his face twisting in exaggerated displeasure. "You know, I really don't like the color. It's so brash and loud. I do have beautiful oriental rugs, though," he added eagerly, as if the idea would be a perfect alternative. "I'd be happy to hang one in every window if it would please the Führer." He held out the flag to hand it back to the man.

"That will not be necessary," the soldier said coldly, now aware that Georg was teasing him. "Keep the flag, Captain, and I strongly suggest that you reconsider your decision. Every house should be displaying the flag before the Führer arrives—and that means *every* house. I'm sure you understand." With a final hard look at Georg, who looked calmly back at him, the officer saluted with another "Heil, Hitler!" and drove away.

With the threat of the Gestapo hanging over their heads now, Maria moved through her days in an anxious daze. Georg was standing up for the country he loved, and she admired and respected him for it, but she was afraid in a way she had never been before. Every time the telephone or doorbell rang, she trembled with fear until she learned the name of the caller. It always turned out to be a friend, but she knew that it was only a matter of time before the enemy would confront them once more.

Then, one day, it did.

"Mother, my new teacher wants to speak to you at school," Lorli announced when she returned home from school a few days later. Maria eyed her curiously. Lorli didn't know what it was about but seemed oddly proud, not worried as the other children would have been. Maria found out the reason the next day.

"Good day, Baroness von Trapp," said the first-grade teacher, a young woman who had replaced the previous teacher only a week ago as part of the nationwide transition to the Nazi education system. "I must ask you to speak to Lorli and help her understand, or you will get into very serious trouble soon."

"What has she done?" asked Maria.

"Yesterday we practiced our new national anthem, which I've been teaching the class," explained the teacher, "but Lorli kept her mouth tightly closed, even after I encouraged her to sing. I thought she might just be shy. When I finally asked her why she wouldn't sing, she said—out loud in front of the whole class—that her father said he would drink ground glass in his tea or finish his life on a dung heap before he ever sang that song!"

Maria choked back a laugh, for she could just picture Lorli repeating his words, complete with her little fist smashing against her other hand, as Georg had done. Laughing, she knew, was the last response she should make if she wanted to avoid trouble.

The teacher smiled apologetically, as if understanding how difficult changes were for some people to make. Her eyes were stern, though, and Maria's heart sank. She said to Maria, "I'm sorry, but next time I will have to report this. I'm sure you understand. It is my patriotic and professional duty."

~

In late May a specialist in Munich delivered devastating news to Maria and Georg. Their unborn baby would probably not survive within her womb. It was time to prepare themselves for a miscarriage, the third since Lorli's birth.

Maria and Georg left the doctor's office subdued, determined to trust God but unable to cast aside their anxiety. As they stepped into the sunny afternoon, Maria stopped and took a deep breath. "Georg, let's do something to take our minds off this for a little while. I have an idea. I've been wanting to see the House of German Art, which recently opened here. Have you heard of it? It's run by the Nazis, but I hear it's worth seeing; and it will while away the afternoon until it's time for our train home."

Georg shrugged his consent, and after asking for directions they discovered that the museum was in the neighborhood. Within ten minutes they arrived at the small building, which was surrounded by bright red geraniums. Maria had always loved them. The art inside, however, horrified them both. Slowly they passed before each painting, each cruder and more brutal than the last, until they came to a wall-sized painting of Hitler himself, the great Führer of the Third Reich. He sat on horseback, clad in armor and holding a long sword. When Georg realized that each viewer was expected to salute the portrait and cry "Heil Hitler!", he stopped.

"I can't do it," he said. "Let's go back the other way."

Maria followed him out the door and suddenly gasped in delight. "Georg, do you smell that? It's frankfurters! I haven't had any for ages. Let's get some! Are you hungry?"

Just outside the exhibition, Maria saw a small restaurant and led Georg inside. It was unusually quiet and clear of cigarette smoke. Assuming this was a stroke of good luck, they sat down. As they pondered the menu, the waiter came to take their order. Before they could speak, he leaned down and whispered, "Have you seen him?"

Maria frowned. "Who?"

"The Führer!" the waiter nearly squealed in his excitement. "Don't look now, but he is at the next table! You are truly honored today to be near him!"

Maria and Georg cautiously peeked toward the table the waiter was pointing to and saw that it was true. There, only a few feet away, sat Adolf Hitler, leader of the Third Reich, sipping raspberry juice with some of his beer-guzzling officers. Georg narrowed his eyes at Maria, as if to indicate that he would like nothing better than to leave, but they certainly could not do so now. Their distaste for Hitler would be plain, and that could endanger them both.

Throughout their meal, they could only sit there as if it didn't matter at all that the conqueror of their beloved homeland sat within speaking distance. At first Maria tried to ignore Hitler and enjoy her frankfurters and mustard, but after a while she started to steal glances at him. How strange, she thought. The great and mighty Führer, who governed the lives of every German and Austrian, was such an ordinary-looking man. He laughed loudly, spoke crudely, and ate as though he were a commoner. He didn't have the noble bearing Georg did, and she wondered if he had even attended a university. Without his uniformed officers around him, he would have blended in with the rest of the customers.

No one could have guessed by looking at him that beneath his tailored brown waistcoat beat a heart bent on power at any cost. He wanted a society where no citizen had guaranteed civil rights and where anyone he didn't like—especially the Jews, God's chosen people —could be sent to grim concentration camps to live under harsh and inhumane conditions. This was the face of evil, Maria suddenly realized with a shock, and it looked just like everyone else. For a moment she felt sick, the food in her mouth tasting like wet sawdust.

"Georg," she said once she was able to swallow, "I'm ready to leave now. Please."

Georg nodded in understanding. "Let's walk through the English Garden nearby," he suggested. "I think that will be much more pleasant."

When they stepped outside, Maria stopped and took several deep breaths of fragrant spring air. Slowly her nausea ebbed as Georg gently led her toward the beautiful park, where the English Garden was celebrating spring in a riot of color.

"Well, what is this?" muttered Georg, patting his breast pocket. He drew out a white envelope. "Oh, I'd forgotten that Hans handed me this the other day." He ripped it open and began to read. Then he froze in his tracks.

"Maria, read this!" He handed her the letter, which asked: "Would Commander Trapp be interested in taking over one of the brand-new submarines and establishing a submarine base in the Adriatic Sea and later in the Mediterranean?"

"Georg, the Nazis are offering you a command?"

Georg's eyes clouded over as he remembered his glorious past as a war hero. "It's been so long . . . it's the chance of a lifetime! Of course I must accept the commission."

Maria said nothing; she was not sure she trusted herself to say the right thing. She knew how much Georg's career as a submarine commander meant to him, but she didn't want him to go to sea, and especially not under the command of Adolf Hitler.

A woman came around beside him on the path and gave him an angry glance, for she had nearly bumped into him, but Georg didn't notice. "But what do they mean by 'later in the Mediterranean'?" he mused. Then it hit him. "That would mean war, Maria." He turned to her, his face stricken with dismay. "I can't command a submarine for the Nazis. How could I live with myself? The idea is out of the question. Absolutely not possible."

Maria nodded, trying not to show her relief, and they continued along the path.

"On the other hand," Georg said, "being a naval officer is my job, and Hitler is the head of state now. Commanding a submarine is the one thing I know how to do well. Could accepting this commission be the will of God?" He shook the letter impatiently, as if exasperated that he had to make such a difficult decision. "Everyone I know is warning me to jump on board with the new regime, to accept things as they are now and not fight it. There is nothing anyone can do to change it, and they say I must think of my children's future. Right now, I am endangering them by not supporting Hitler. Am I trying to be better than everyone else, at the expense of my own family?"

"I suppose that's possible," admitted Maria. She was about to say more, but a glance at Georg's face stilled her tongue. He was lost in his thoughts, engaged in a personal struggle all his own between himself and

God. She took his hand and squeezed it, swallowing the many words she wanted to say. Inwardly she prayed, "Thy will be done!"

Georg walked slowly, eyes fixed to the ground, while Maria tried to enjoy the brilliant displays of flowers and foliage that surrounded them in the English Garden. Finally, he gave a violent shake of his head and said, "No, I can't do it. I once took an oath on our proud old flag and swore to serve the emperor for God and country. To serve Hitler would go against that oath. I can't—I won't—break it, no matter what. Even if he sends me to a concentration camp. I must be strong."

Soberly, Georg and Maria completed their circuit of the garden and made their way to the train station. They hardly noticed the cheerful bustle of the streets. They were too burdened by the realization that Hitler's power over their lives was growing. How would the Third Reich react when Georg denied the naval commission?

Georg's worries only increased when Rupert met them at the Salzburg station that evening.

"Look what I have!" Rupert cried when he saw them. In his hand he waved a letter. Maria and Georg looked at him anxiously, their hearts sinking. By the strange expression on his face, they both knew it wasn't a letter from a friend. "It's a letter from the biggest hospital in Vienna! I just graduated a week ago, and they are already offering me a position as a doctor. Can you believe it?"

Georg and Maria glanced at each other knowingly as they crossed the train tracks to their back gate. It made perfect sense. The hospital needed doctors, just as law offices needed lawyers and dental practices needed dentists. The Nazis were sending the many Jews who worked in these professions to concentration camps!

"Of course I can't accept it," said Rupert cheerfully, tucking the letter into his coat pocket. "I will never work for Hitler's cause. I haven't even made the 'Heil, Hitler' salute yet, although I'm sure it's only a matter of time before someone notices and demands that I do it."

Georg smiled in relief. "I'm glad to hear it, son."

"My only concern is that I don't know how to word my refusal politely enough—in a way that won't cause them offense. The last thing I want to do is draw attention to myself."

"What will you do to earn your living?" asked Georg. He was proud of Rupert, but the young man still needed a job after graduation.

Rupert shrugged, opening the gate to let them through. "I'll figure it out. God will help me."

The next few days were anxious ones for Georg and Rupert as they delayed sending their refusals, wondering how long they could avoid drawing the Nazis' attention. Then something else happened.

One day, the telephone rang. Because it was Hans' day off, Maria answered it in the library, where she was trying to balance the checkbook—no easy feat during these dark days. Georg was too absorbed with his news-paper to pay much attention, until he realized that Maria said almost nothing to the caller before hanging up, except for, "Thank you so much. I will speak to my husband about it and call you back tomorrow." After writing down the caller's phone number, she hung up and stared pensively at the paper until Georg said, "Is everything all right, my dear?"

Maria looked up at him with troubled eyes. "That was a government official calling on behalf of Hitler."

Georg lifted an eyebrow as Maria cleared her throat. "Georg," she said, "we've been asked to sing for his upcoming birthday celebration."

Georg's mouth fell open. "What? You must be mis-taken, Maria."

Maria shook her head. "I'm afraid not."

For several seconds, Georg couldn't speak at all, only ponder what this opportunity meant.

"What should we do?" Maria gently prompted him. "I must call him back tomorrow. It is quite an honor to be asked."

"Yes, it is. And if we did accept, I'm pretty certain that our money troubles would be over. We would get so many contracts, we wouldn't be able to accept them all."

"It sounds very glamorous and exciting!" said Maria. "And perhaps this is an opportunity to appear some-what favorable to Hitler and thus stay out of trouble."

"Let's discuss it with the children at our family meeting this evening," said Georg.

To the children, though, singing for Hitler seemed like no opportunity at all.

"Will we have to salute the Führer?" asked Johanna.

"Will we have to sing our new national anthem?" asked Martina.

"How will Father Wasner direct us? Hitler hates priests. His officers won't let him in the door," Mitzi pointed out.

"It sounds really exciting, but how can we remain anti-Nazi and accept their money and praise at the same time?" asked Werner.

At this last question, the family fell silent. The answer was clear: the von Trapps could not accept the invitation and stay true to their principles because Hitler and the Nazis were against everything they stood for as both Austrians and Catholics.

"But if we refuse," said Georg slowly, looking at each one in turn, "it will mark the third time we have refused an offer from the Nazis. We can't do it and escape notice much longer. We as a family must make a choice that's harder than any decision we've ever made. We can keep our beloved home and possessions and comfort by agreeing to perform at Hitler's birthday celebration and making the best of it, but we must understand that in doing so, we will give up our spiritual goods. We cannot have both." He looked to Maria for support and found the assurance he needed to continue. "And frankly, children, I'd rather see you poor and struggling to scratch out a living if that's what it costs to remain honest and true to your faith."

The children nodded slowly in tentative agreement, but Georg stopped them with a raised hand. "Before you respond, you all need to hear one thing more. In order to follow our consciences, we must not only give up our material possessions and live in poverty but also leave Austria. Do you understand? We must find a way to escape. It will be too dangerous to stay."

"Where would we go?" asked Agathe.

Maria picked up a piece of paper and showed it to the children. "Do you remember this contract? The one from Charles Wagner in America? It hasn't expired yet. If we sign it, we can escape to America at least for the concert season. Father Wasner would probably come with us, too. He is also in a dangerous position. If he comes with us, he could continue to direct our concerts."

"At the end of the concert season, we may be able to return home without the Nazis noticing," added Georg. "Or maybe the situation will have changed in Europe."

Werner spoke immediately. "Yes, Papa, let's do it. I don't see that we have much of a choice, and we know America is safe." He looked to his brothers and sisters for support, and they nodded in agreement.

"Well," said Georg, "Mother and I have much to

think about. Thank you all for your strength of character, and your courage."

It took only a quick telephone call to persuade Father Wasner to join them, but as a priest he needed the archbishop to release him from his duties. The next morning Georg and Maria asked for an audience with the archbishop at his palace in Salzburg.

"Your Excellency," began Georg respectfully after kissing the archbishop's episcopal ring, "my wife and I are here to seek your spiritual wisdom about a very delicate matter. In fact, this is a secret, so we ask you to keep it just between us."

The archbishop nodded gravely and listened as Georg explained the danger the family and Father Wasner faced and their hope that he could be released from his duties during the summer to accompany them to America.

"I and all the children except Rupert are actually Italian citizens, Your Excellency," added Georg as a final plea, "because my first wife and I were living in Trieste when Italy claimed it after the Great War. I don't think the Nazis would arrest me, even if I refuse the commission. However, my son Rupert repatriated to Austria when he became a medical student in Innsbruck, and both Maria and Father Wasner are also Austrian citizens. I am afraid the Nazis would take revenge for my refusal by harming them."

The archbishop considered their request in silence, his eyes closed in concentration and prayer, his brow furrowed by concern and uncertainty. Finally, he opened his eyes and said, "I will need to consider the matter further. Could you please return tomorrow at the same time?"

Georg and Maria agreed and left, worried that the archbishop would say no. The next day, their fears were relieved when he greeted them with a relaxed smile. He wasted no time in assuring them that their request was granted. "In fact, I tell you this as your bishop, that the will of God is that you leave Austria as soon as you are able and take Father Wasner with you. Somehow, I feel . . ." He paused and raised his eyes to the dome of the cathedral outside his window, his face suddenly serious. "Somehow I feel that in addition to protecting you all, this decision may prove valuable to the whole diocese someday." Then he smiled again into their eyes and raised a hand in blessing. "Do not be afraid, my children. God will never abandon you, no matter how far you may roam. Just remember to keep your eyes on Him with every step you take."

II

ESCAPE TO AMERICA

August 1938

L EAVING AUSTRIA WAS NOT EASY, for the von Trapps
and Father Wasner had many decisions and plans
to make once Georg and Maria turned down the invitation to sing at Hitler's birthday party. In addition, new
performance costumes had to be made for everyone
because the old ones would not last another concert
season. Because they were the commonly worn *Dirndl*

dresses for the women and wool suits for the men, they would also serve as traveling clothes. No one would notice anything amiss if they wore them daily.

They needed to figure out how to travel to America, which would be a long and difficult journey no matter what they decided to do. Obtaining visas that would allow them to stay in America for an entire concert season was yet another challenge. The complications were overwhelming, but time was of the essence. It wouldn't be long before Georg would be forced to accept the naval commission.

One early August afternoon, Hans said, "Captain, Baroness . . . may I have just a moment?"

"Of course, Hans," said Georg, as he and Maria turned to give the butler their attention.

Hans cleared his throat and came closer. "Captain," he said again, this time in a low, urgent voice, his eyes shifting around the hall as if to make sure that no boarding guests were nearby, "I must warn you of something. It could cost me dearly if anyone finds out that I told you, so please take my warning seriously and do not share it with anyone."

"Of course, Hans," promised Georg. "Let's go into the library, where you can speak privately."

Georg led Maria and Hans into the library and shut the door. Hans continued, carefully choosing his words. "As you know, I am a party member, and I am honored to be one. But I have also served you for many years, and you have been good to me. I know you are thinking of leaving Austria because of the dangers you face by opposing the Führer. Out of loyalty to you, I must tell you that if you don't leave right away, you won't be able to leave at all. The borders will be closing very soon, and you will not be able to hide easily anywhere in Austria. Nazi soldiers are being stationed everywhere, even deep in the mountains."

Georg stared at Hans in dismay. He had not considered border closings. "Are you sure, Hans? I haven't heard any rumors. Usually news like this has a way of—"

"Very sure, Captain," interrupted Hans. "Please take my advice. I wouldn't want anything to happen to you."

Georg nodded. "I will, Hans. Thank you. And thank you for your kindness and loyalty. I know this was difficult for you."

"Yes, Captain, but I will help you in whatever way I can. I know you will soon need to dismiss the remaining staff, including me, but I'll help until then."

The family and Father Wasner flew into action. Georg and Maria had not yet sent the contract to Mr. Wagner, reluctant to make any firm commitments too soon, but now they mailed it immediately, along with a letter asking for an advance of the money they would make in order to buy ship passage. In the letter they also directed him to reply to an inn in Sankt Georgen (San Giorgio), Italy. Since Georg and his children were declared Italian citizens after World War I, it made sense to find refuge in Italy. And a friend had once recommended Sankt Georgen, right across the border, as an inexpensive place to stay for a summer vacation. There they would wait for Mr. Wagner's instructions.

There was much to be done to prepare twelve people —the family and Father Wasner—to travel across the ocean for a concert tour, and they could hardly move fast enough. Instruments and music were packed carefully, and the house was rented to a group of priests who had been displaced from their communal home by the Nazis. To keep from raising suspicion among their friends, all of whom were loyal to Hitler, Georg and Maria also began telling everyone excitedly about their upcoming trip to Italy. Finally, with much sadness and gratitude, the family had to say good-bye to Hans the butler, the two laundry assistants, and Resi the cook.

When the day for their departure arrived, the family picked up their knapsacks and suitcases and for the last time walked through the garden to the little gate at the back of the estate, where they had first entered it many years ago. They each turned to gaze sadly at the stately villa and its garden, woods, and park, wondering if they would ever see it again. Then they made their way over the tracks and onto the morning train headed south to Italy.

The next day, the newspapers announced that the borders of Austria had closed.

~

Despite the family's anxiety about receiving Mr. Wagner's reply, life in Sankt Georgen was pleasant. Meadows and mountains surrounded the charming Alpine village, and their accommodations were quite comfortable. Also, the move had brought a financial boon to the family. After World War I, Captain von Trapp briefly served the Italian government, which had absorbed the ports and the ships of the defeated Austrian Empire. The Italian government owed the captain some money for this service, which it refused to pay while he was living in Austria. As the von Trapps waited in Italy for Mr. Wagner's reply, Georg finally collected the money that was owed him. God was truly providing for the family, just as the archbishop had assured them He would. From this Georg and Maria took their strength, trusting that all would be well.

In early autumn, a large envelope from Mr. Wagner arrived from that magical place called America. With trembling fingers Georg opened it before the family at dinner and pulled out twelve tickets—enough for Georg, Maria, each of the nine children, and Father Wasner.

"We're going to America!" Maria cried, jumping up from the table and clapping her hands in excitement. Everyone cheered.

Once again, the family packed their knapsacks and suitcases. They first took a train to Switzerland, and from there they traveled through the Alps and across France to the Atlantic coast, where they boarded a ferry that took them through the choppy waters of the English Channel to Dover, England. Wearily, they boarded another train for London—and then yet another train to the southern coast at Southampton. Finally, on October 7, 1938, the von Trapps boarded the passenger and cargo ship named the *American Farmer* and left their old lives far behind them.

Soon after they waved to the rocky English coast, a storm whipped up, causing so many passengers to be seasick that the dining room was nearly empty for three days! None of the children or Father Wasner could do anything but groan in their beds. Georg, used to the moods of the sea, nursed them all, while Maria obeyed his instructions to stay in their cabin. Their new little one was due in just a few months, and Maria had to take extra-good care of herself. She expected to be seasick like the others but instead found herself only bored and hungry.

When the storm was over, she emerged from the cabin with a plan of action. Why be lazy for two weeks waiting for New York City to appear over the horizon when they had a whole new language to learn? Armed with a notebook and a pen, Maria set to work learning English.

"Vat is fat, please?" Maria politely asked every English-speaking passenger she could find, pointing to an object. "A watch," the person might say with a smile, or "a spoon." She wrote down what she heard in her notebook, not bothering with spellings: *e votsch, e spuhn.* Gradually, her list grew, and when she proudly showed Georg her new words, he raised an eyebrow but said nothing. Undeterred, Maria kept learning whatever English she could. An English actress named Miss Powell helped Maria work on her pronunciation, so that instead of saying "vat" for *what*, she learned to say "hoo-wat" instead.

An American doctor also tried to help by giving Maria private lessons in American slang and money. Other American passengers taught them two folk songs to add to their repertoire: "My Old Kentucky Home" and "Old Black Joe." By the end of the voyage, the von Trapps and Father Wasner had already come to know Americans as kind, generous, and helpful.

The morning of their arrival, the von Trapps and Father Wasner gripped the railing of the ship in excitement as the skyscrapers of Manhattan emerged from the fog. Then they saw the most breathtaking vision of all. Standing proudly and shining like a beacon of hope, the Statue of Liberty welcomed them to America!

What a sight the von Trapps made as they disembarked at New York Harbor later that day! With their European costumes, accompanying priest, and fifty-six pieces of luggage full of personal items, music, baby supplies, and instruments, everyone waiting on land forgot the passengers they came to meet as they craned their necks to get a better view of the spectacle coming down the gangplank.

New York City was quite a sight for the von Trapps, too. The throngs of pedestrians, cars, and buses and the deafening subway noises were an overwhelming cacophony after the more subdued sounds of Salzburg, Sankt Georgen, and even London. Everywhere there was activity and color and rushing cars and tall, narrow buildings—taller than anything they had ever seen in Europe. But it was the people that amazed them the most. It seemed as if all of Europe had shown up to greet them, and even some of Asia and Africa! The faces of New York City were of the entire world.

One face in the crowd pushed forward with a joyful shout, and a card soared high above it with the words "Trapp Family Choir" printed in bold, black letters. "Hello, hello, von Trapps!" shouted a man's voice. Georg and Maria stopped, trying to find the person in the throbbing crowd who called their name.

"There he is!" cried Martina, pointing to a short, balding man with glasses and a broad smile. "Do you see him, Papa?"

Finally, Georg's eyes found the sign's owner, and his eyes brightened with relief. "Ah!" he cried as he approached the man, who tucked the card under his arm and grabbed Georg's hand in both of his.

"Captain von Trapp!" he cried, his face beaming with delight. Then he turned to Maria and grabbed her hand in welcome as well. "Baroness! Welcome to

America! Welcome! My name is Mr. Snowden. I am Charles Wagner's assistant."

Rupert, Agathe, and Georg already knew some English, so they quickly translated for the rest of the family. Everyone shook his hand and made introductions. After momentary amazement at their many pieces of luggage, Mr. Snowden cheerfully arranged for the bags' transport to the hotel and directed everyone into nearby limousines hired by the agency. Although he couldn't speak German and no one in the von Trapp family was yet fluent enough to translate every word he said, they nevertheless managed to have a jolly conversation of sorts all the way to the hotel.

Finally, the limousines pulled up to a skyscraper so high that the von Trapps could not see the top. Maria slowly sounded out "Hotel Wellington." This would be their home for at least a week, they eventually learned, as they settled in and prepared for their concert tour. Until then, they were free to explore.

America was a land of wonders the likes of which the von Trapps had never seen. Never had they been higher than five floors, and now they were on the nineteenth! Never had they sat at a drugstore counter for lunch (nor ever seen a drugstore!), or eaten sandwiches as large as their hands, or seen dark-skinned elevator operators, or navigated a town by its numbered streets, or ridden a subway or an escalator. They visited the library, Central Park, and even Macy's department store. Everywhere they looked they encountered something new and exciting, and almost everyone they met welcomed them with open arms and broad smiles.

After several days, the family and Father Wasner could roam the neighborhood around the hotel with ease, and Maria had found a convent boarding school for Lorli and Rosmarie—the Ursuline Academy in the Bronx. Since the little girls could not sing with the family and needed to go to school, this seemed the safest place for them. Poor Lorli and Rosmarie! Despite their tears and sobs, Georg and Maria resolutely said good-bye and turned their eyes toward their concert tour, praying they would be all right. It was one of the hardest things Maria had ever done.

One day, a big chartered bus painted royal blue pulled up in front of the Hotel Wellington. The words *Special Coach* and *Trapp Family Choir* marched across the sides. For the next few months, the bus would be home. Everyone boarded it with excitement, piling in the enormous load of luggage and arguing over who would have which seat. In the back of the bus was a narrow cot for anyone who needed to lie down, and in the front sat smiling, gentlemanly Mr. Tallerie.

Their first concert was in Pennsylvania at Lafayette College, and Mr. Wagner and all his office staff came to see them. Of course, this made the von Trapps very nervous, for what if Mr. Wagner regretted ever bringing them here? But gradually his tense expression relaxed into a smile of pleasure as the audience rewarded them with hearty applause—and then it was on to Virginia, Ohio, Alabama, Tennessee, and Illinois. They sang Bach, Handel, Mozart, and more of the finest music of Europe, and audiences everywhere listened appreciatively and welcomed them with warm applause. The after-concert receptions were the hardest, especially for Georg, for during these they had to shake hands and greet hundreds of people—which was quite a feat, of course, when English was still a mystery to most of them.

By December they were at last on the way back to New York City, where they would pick up Rosmarie and Lorli from their boarding school and enjoy a well-earned Christmas rest before continuing on their way to the Northeast for more concerts. It was during the break that Georg, Maria, and Father Wasner met with Mr. Wagner for coffee one evening to share their adventures with him and discuss the remainder of the season.

"You have been a remarkable success," he said warmly in German after hearing how the concerts had gone. "I'm sure the people in New England will enjoy your concerts, too, especially in Boston."

Georg nodded. "We have heard of Boston. I, for one, am looking forward to seeing some of the historical sights there."

"I am, too," agreed Maria, "but I will be especially happy when the baby is finally here."

Mr. Wagner nearly dropped his coffee cup as he bolted upright in his chair. "A baby?" he repeated. "Whose baby?"

Georg and Maria exchanged glances. "Well . . . mine," replied Maria cautiously.

"No one told me anything about a baby being on the way!" exclaimed the old bachelor.

Maria glanced at her ample stomach. True, she wore voluminous blouses and skirts, but how could he not have known by now? It was so obvious!

"Is something wrong, Mr. Wagner?" asked Father Wasner.

"A baby . . . a baby . . . ," spluttered Mr. Wagner, his face beginning to turn a little red. "I can't have a newborn baby touring with you!"

"Why not?" asked Maria irritably, throwing up her hands. "I am quite healthy, and I have no reason to suspect that the baby won't be."

"No! I can't have that," insisted Mr. Wagner. "I must have you focused on your concerts, and with all the traveling ahead, a newborn could cause problems . . . complications. No," he said again, shaking his head firmly, "this will not work. I do wish you'd told me before you sailed."

Georg set down his cup, realizing that Mr. Wagner was truly upset. "We didn't think it would cause such concern. With so many of us, the baby will be well cared for, and we can hire a nanny if needed."

"No, no," said Mr. Wagner, holding up his hand as

if to prevent any more arguments. "No newborn babies on this tour. We will have to cancel the remaining
concerts. I am sorry, but this is my policy."

Despite Maria's iron will and impassioned pleadings,
as well as Father Wasner's and Georg's well-reasoned
arguments, nothing would change the manager's mind,
and with that the von Trapps' first American concert
tour came to an abrupt end. Mr. Wagner quickly took
his leave after promising that their final payment would
be delivered the next day.

For a long time, Georg, Maria, and Father Wasner
sat miserably in the coffee shop and discussed their
options. Their visas didn't expire until March. What
would they do until then? They couldn't afford to live
in a hotel without a steady income. Why would God
have brought them here only to let such a disaster happen? It seemed He had abandoned them after all.

In dejected silence, Maria, Georg, and Father Wasner walked back to the hotel. None of them had any
idea what to do next. The final check Mr. Wagner had
promised them would carry them for a few weeks, but
after that they would have no income. They couldn't
return to the Villa Trapp with the Nazis in power, but
they had no more concerts scheduled. The U.S. government wouldn't allow them to earn money any other
way with the kind of visas they had, and then there
was the baby on the way . . .

Despite her resolve to trust God and be strong, tears
filled Maria's eyes as they entered the grand hotel. She

knew how expensive it was. They needed to find something else immediately, but where could they afford
to house twelve people—and soon a newborn baby?
Would they be sleeping in the alleyways of New York
City, surrounded by all their luggage? Would her baby
be born in a park or a public restroom? Her dramatic
imagination began to spin until she was choking back
sobs. Georg wrapped his arm around her kindly and
steered her toward the elevator. "It will be all right, my
dear," he assured her. "We can't lose hope already."

"But all this time we thought God was with us!"
wailed Maria. "Now it turns out He hasn't been at all.
Coming here was a big mistake, and we just *thought* we
were following His will! How could we have been so
foolish?"

Suddenly a shrill voice cut through the quiet lobby.
"Baroness von Trapp!"

Maria quickly rubbed the tears from her eyes and
turned toward the voice. A tall, broad-shouldered
woman in a mink coat strode toward them from the
front desk. Maria and Georg regarded her curiously,
for they had never seen her before. The woman held
her hand out with a warm smile and shook hands with
the three of them, saying in perfect German, "Hello,
Captain von Trapp, Father Wasner. I know you don't
know me, but I recognize you from pictures, and I
believe you know my daughter—Yella Pessl. Do you
remember her?"

Maria and Georg brightened with recognition. "Ah yes!" cried Maria. "We certainly do!"

"Of course, the famous harpsichordist from Vienna," agreed Georg. "We've met her on several occasions. Delightful young woman."

"And so encouraging of us, too, when we were just getting started with our singing," added Maria. "How is she now? Is she still performing in Austria?"

"Oh no, no, no," said Mrs. Pessl. "She is here now, performing in America. Right now, she is with the New York Philharmonic."

"How wonderful!" cried Maria, throwing her arms exuberantly into the air. "I'm so glad to hear that. Vienna is poorer without her, I'm sure."

"Well, what are you doing here?" demanded Mrs. Pessl. "I had not heard you were in town. Are you giving concerts?"

When all three faces fell at the same moment, Mrs. Pessl clapped her hand to her mouth. "Oh dear, I've said something wrong. I'm so sorry."

Maria shook her head and placed a comforting hand on the woman's arm. "No, no, it's all right. It's just that . . ." She cleared her throat, uncertain of what to share with this woman they had just met.

Father Wasner spoke up. "We were in the middle of an entire season that took us all over the country, but our manager just canceled the second half only an hour ago. We are just returning from that meeting."

"I'm having a baby in a few weeks," added Maria, "and he said that newborns are against his policy."

Mrs. Pessl recoiled. "But that's awful! What a horrible man! What will you do now?"

Georg shrugged. "We don't know. Our visas don't expire until March, and Hitler has control of Austria. We can't go back, but we have no other source of income."

"That's simply *awful*!" cried Mrs. Pessl with passion. "I am so sorry." She paused, thinking hard. Then she said, "Well, there is only one thing to do if you want to earn a living wage with your singing here in America."

"What is that?" asked Maria eagerly.

"You must give a Town Hall concert. Every artist who wants to be successful must do that. If you make it at the Town Hall, you can go anywhere in America. You will need a publicity agent."

"A what?" asked Georg blankly.

"A publicity agent." Her eyes widened in dismay. "Don't you have someone do your publicity for you?"

Georg and Maria glanced at each other. "To do what for us?" asked Maria timidly.

Clapping her hand over her mouth again, Mrs. Pessl gazed at them in dumbfounded amazement. Then she seemed to burst into life. "Publicity! You know, to make people aware of who you are and interest them in attending your concerts. Oh my goodness, this is just terrible! Where's the telephone?" Twisting her head this way and that with an air of urgency, her eyes finally spotted the lobby telephone booth. With a stern "Don't move!" she scurried into it and banged the door shut, leaving Maria, Georg, and Father Wasner staring.

In a few moments she returned, her face smiling but her eyes burning with purpose. "All right, it's all set. Yella's publicity agent will be here in just a half hour, and then we'll sit and talk. We'll get you all fixed up for your last three months in America, don't you worry! Now, I'm going to go upstairs and put away my hat and coat, and then I'll rejoin you for coffee in the lounge. Miss Behrens will find us there. Until then!" With a little wave, Mrs. Pessl turned around and disappeared.

~

The next couple of weeks passed in a surreal blur as the publicity agent, Miss Behrens, went to work putting the von Trapps in the public eye. Every day, they had the strange experience of seeing a newly published article about themselves, often with photos of them doing the most ordinary activities—eating at a Chinese restaurant, window shopping on Fifth Avenue, boarding a trolley car. Then reporters came to interview them for the *Times*, *Life* magazine, the *Herald Tribune*, and more. Their singing was of surprisingly little interest to the reporters, and the von Trapps found themselves uncomfortably answering personal questions such as "Why do you wear those funny dresses?"

and "Why did you leave Europe?" What did it matter? they wondered. They were here to share their music! Yet the questions continued, until the family was sick of the whole thing.

Yet the publicity worked, and the Town Hall concert was nearly sold out. This was their chance to show America what they could do. Would people like them? What would the reviewers say? Would any new managers step forward to offer them contracts? Success at this concert would make all the difference. Positive reviews would be the beginning of a successful musical career in America. They might even make millions!

With this hope shining before them, the Trapp Family Choir sang their hearts out with three very difficult madrigals and Bach's entire forty-five-minute *Jesu, Meine Freude* ("Jesus, My Joy"). Georg sat near the back of the auditorium to watch the audience's reactions, leaning forward with his fingers templed pensively at his lips.

Immediately after the concert, the family felt deflated. Georg had noticed many people leaving before the end of the concert. Some of those appeared to be reviewers or curious managers from various agencies, not the music-loving patrons they hoped to draw. Maybe the concert hadn't been successful at all.

Then a tall young man rushed backstage and grabbed Maria's hands. She jumped in alarm, but then she saw the tears in his eyes. Smiling, she said in careful English, "Hello, thank you for attending the concert! Did you enjoy it?"

The young man smiled through his tears and nodded emphatically. "Oh yes," he said breathlessly. "Mrs. von Trapp, I want to tell you that I am sure that your performance of Bach's motet was exactly as he would have wanted it. Beautiful, really, just exquisite!"

"Well, thank you much," said Maria, trying not to show her confusion as some of the children gathered around her to listen. Her English was quickly improving, but she didn't know what *exactly* or *exquisite* meant. "Is very wonderful to hear kind words."

"Thank *you* for your glorious concert," replied the young man, his face beaming with delight. "You must come to see me at the library sometime. My name is Carlton Smith. I would love to introduce you to my colleagues—er, fellow employees. Please come anytime!" With that, he spread a smile around the whole family and then left.

Everyone felt better after that, but they still had a long night to sleep through before they would learn their fate in the morning's newspapers. If the reviews were poor, then all was lost in America. They would have to go back to Europe and stay there. If they were positive, though . . . oh, it was almost too much to hope for!

The next morning Miss Behrens, Yella, and Mrs. Pessl rushed into the hotel while the von Trapps were coming down to breakfast. In their hands they excitedly waved stacks of newspapers. "They are wonderful!" cried Mrs. Pessl, not caring who heard her. "You must read them right away!"

At the breakfast table, the papers were passed around to everyone's increasing delight.

"We're like no other family alive!" cried Martina, pointing to a column.

"Music achieved one of its miracles," read Werner.

"All-around musicianship," Yella translated in German, knowing such words would be beyond them in English, "and exceedingly refined!"

Everyone was so happy that it was difficult to eat their rolls, butter, and coffee. The von Trapps were a success! Now, anything could happen in this wonderful land called America.

~

Georg, Maria, and some of the children decided to honor Carlton Smith's invitation to visit him at the nearby library, where he worked at the circulation desk. When they arrived, Carlton was talking to a tall, distinguished-looking man. He caught sight of them, and his face brightened immediately.

"It's the von Trapps!" he cried, forgetting that one must be quiet in a library, especially the staff. "I can't believe it! I was just talking about you to Professor Albrecht here. He is from the University of Pennsylvania in Philadelphia, and he also happens to speak German."

After making introductions, Carlton asked, "The professor is a music lover himself, so I would like him to attend one of your concerts. What are your plans? Do you have any more concerts scheduled that he can attend while he's here?"

Georg shook his head with an apologetic smile. "I'm afraid not. We hope to schedule more, but right now we must find a place to live until our visas expire in early March. The hotel where we've been living has become too expensive for us."

"Aha!" said Professor Albrecht, pointing one finger into the air as if to mark his next words. "I know just the place for you, if you are willing to move. There is a furnished house for rent near my own house in Philadelphia. It's a little small for so many people, but it is clean and in good repair with a kind landlady. I understand that it is only a hundred dollars a month. Would you be interested?"

Maria regarded the professor with awe. Here they were in the library visiting Carlton, a man they had only recently met and might have easily forgotten, and just by chance he was speaking with Professor Albrecht, who just by chance knew of an affordable house they could rent! Taking Georg's hand, she looked solemnly into his eyes and said softly, "I am so ashamed, Georg.

The next time I doubt God's care for us, please remind me of this moment."

"If you'll remind me as well, when I doubt Him," replied Georg with an understanding smile. "Such a coincidence could only come from heaven."

12

MINSTRELS OF ELLIS ISLAND

December 1938

T HE HOUSE IN PHILADELPHIA was all that the professor had claimed it would be—inexpensive, clean,
well kept, furnished, and indeed quite small for twelve
people. After the spacious Villa Trapp, it felt very
cramped. As the von Trapps and Father Wasner settled in, however, they experienced American hospi-
tality in ways that touched them deeply. From the

moment they arrived, strangers kept stopping by to deliver useful items—lamps, dishes, blankets, and even a Victrola with records so that they could fill the house with music.

Most of these kind strangers were Quakers, which the von Trapps knew in Europe as the Society of Friends. They were known for helping others and had, in fact, helped provide Austrians with food during a famine they had suffered during World War I. Because of them, Maria had survived that famine.

Professor Albrecht also introduced them to his friends, including Mr. and Mrs. Drinker, a couple who had such a passionate love for music that once a month they held a party where the guests sang a variety of songs a cappella and enjoyed supper together. Despite their shaky English, the von Trapps had a wonderful time at the party; they even performed a piece upon request. They left fast friends with the Drinkers, and their friendship would last the rest of their lives.

It was in the light and warmth of these new friendships that the von Trapps spent their first Christmas in America. Though the day was quiet, it was peaceful and blessed with even more generosity from their friends—baskets of groceries and sweets, books and records and toys. They even had real candles for their small Christmas tree, just as they had in Austria.

A few weeks after Christmas came the most beautiful, most precious gift of all. Little Johannes was born, and the family prayed the rosary and sang hymns in thanksgiving for his safe arrival. Yes, the little house was small, but it was rich in love and blessings.

As March 4 drew near, the family again grew anxious. That was the day their American visas would expire. If they did not have concerts to sing, they would have to return to Europe. Such an idea was unthinkable with Hitler conquering everything in his path.

Then one day, their new friends had an idea. "Why not apply for a visa extension?" suggested Mr. Drinker. "You have a way to earn income if you can find another concert agent, so I'm sure it would be nothing more than a formality."

"With the threat of war in Europe, I can't imagine they would turn you down," added Mrs. Drinker.

With newfound hope, Georg and Maria immediately submitted their visa extension application, and the family began to pray for the government to approve it in time.

Meanwhile, Mr. Wagner surprised them with another offer for a concert tour, which would begin in September. Since Johannes would no longer be a newborn, Mr. Wagner didn't mind him so much. Until September, if they were very careful with their money and could perform at least once a month, they could survive in the little Philadelphia house.

Several weeks passed, and on a cold, dreary day in

February an official letter from the U.S. government arrived.

"I'm afraid to open it," said Georg, waving the envelope as the family gathered around the dining table. Professor Albrecht, who had been invited to dinner, asked, "What is it, Georg?"

"I think it's the reply from the government about our visa extension." He held out the letter. "Will you read it for us, Professor? We'll all be sure to understand it that way."

The professor ripped open the envelope, unfolded the single piece of stationery, and read it slowly, first in English and then translating it into German. The letter was brief but firm. The U.S. government had denied their application for a visa extension. Hitler or no Hitler, contract or no contract, the von Trapps and Father Wasner would have to sail back across the ocean to Europe. Their American adventures seemed to be over.

When the professor finished, everyone but slumbering Johannes sat dumbstruck. The denial was so unexpected and the disappointment so painful that no one could think of anything to say.

"I . . . I don't understand," Agathe finally said in a small voice. "Why did they turn us down?"

The professor read it again and shook his head. "The letter isn't clear, but it seems to suggest that you might be a danger to the United States because of the trouble in Europe. I'm really not sure, though."

"Because we speak the same language Hitler does? But all we do is give concerts!" protested Martina.

"These are difficult times," said Professor Albrecht sadly. "I'm so sorry. Not only for your own sakes, but selfishly for myself and the Drinkers and all of those who have come to know you. Everyone wants you to stay."

Maria patted his arm comfortingly. "You're very kind, Professor. We will truly miss you and all those who have made us feel so welcome here." She turned to Georg. "Will you go to the ticket office tomorrow, then?"

He nodded slowly. "Yes, I suppose I'll have to. It will take nearly every dime we've got, I'm afraid."

"Where will we go?" asked Werner. "We can't go back home."

Georg sighed. "No, that would be too dangerous now, at least for us men. We would almost certainly be forced to serve in the military. And there would be no warm welcome for the rest of the family—we burned all our bridges behind us when we left. I'll have to think about where we should go. Father Wasner, do you have any ideas?"

The quiet priest considered for a moment. "I saw an advertisement in the newspaper just yesterday for a ship that will be leaving the day our visas expire— the *Normandie*. It will dock at Southampton, England. I don't know what we'd do once we got there, but at least the country will be safe. Hitler hasn't reached it yet, and they are allies with the United States. Maybe they would accept us as refugees and allow us to stay for a while."

"Maybe we can schedule some concerts there," suggested Hedwig hopefully.

"We'd need an agent," Rupert reminded her. "You know that."

"Well, we could get one!" retorted Hedwig.

"Maybe," said Georg with a nod and an agreeable smile, but his eyes were troubled. Caring for his family now seemed impossible and so did trusting that God would take care of them yet again.

Maria seemed to read his thoughts. "Remember," she said quietly, leaning close to him, "the miracle of this house."

Georg frowned and then gave a wan smile. He whispered, "You're right. We promised we'd remind each other, didn't we?" Louder, he addressed the whole family. "Let's not lose heart. Remember how God has taken care of all our needs every single time. We must trust that He will this time, too. Father Wasner, will you lead us in a prayer to help restore our spirits and to ask for God's help?"

The next three days were long and dreary as the family and Father Wasner tried to trust God to provide for this new and urgent need. Georg managed to secure enough third-class tickets on the *Normandie* for March 4, which gave him some relief. Just as he had feared, though, the purchase took nearly all the family's money, and no one had come up with any other ideas for what to do once they reached England. Reluctantly, they began to close up the house, and every night they said the rosary as a plea for help. There were only a few weeks left.

Then one evening at the dinner table, Johanna suddenly gave a little shriek and dropped her fork. Everyone jumped.

"What is wrong with you?" demanded Werner, irritated with her for startling him.

Johanna was glowing with smiles despite Werner's rebuke. "I just remembered—the Danish agent!"

For a moment everyone was silent as they searched for the same memory. Then almost at once, everyone but Father Wasner gasped as they realized what she meant.

"You're right!" cried Rupert. "You're a genius, Johanna!"

Father Wasner hadn't quite caught up yet. "The Danish agent?" he asked quizzically.

Agathe nodded. "Yes, don't you remember, Father? He came to visit us last year in Aigen to offer us a concert tour in Scandinavia. I think it was Oslo, Copenhagen, and . . ."

"Stockholm," supplied Maria from the living room. She had jumped up to search for the contract in the envelope they kept in an end table. "Ah, here it is!"

She returned to the dining room waving an envelope. "And it hasn't expired yet!" she said triumphantly.

Georg's face suddenly looked five years younger as he relaxed for the first time since the day of the fateful letter about their visas. With a sigh of relief he said, "I'll wire them a telegram as soon as the office opens tomorrow. Then we must all pray hard that he will still want us."

A telegram across the ocean was expensive, so as the long anxious days of waiting for a reply began, the family began to run low on food. No one wanted to beg their friends for even more help, but it wasn't long before Mrs. Drinker, who loved to take charge of situations, noticed that their cupboards were nearly empty when Maria made her a cup of tea one day. Quickly, their friends rallied to help and reminded the family again of God's faithfulness.

The days passed so slowly that the family sometimes felt as if they were moving through water. All anyone could think about was whether the reply from the Danish agent would arrive before the *Normandie* departed on March 4. Rosmarie and Lorli continued with school as usual, but even they understood the heavy burden that weighed upon the family.

The family continued to pack, but in grave silence. If an offer from the Danish agent failed to arrive in time, they would have to beg the British government for help or sing on the streets for a few coins. Was that really the plan God had in mind for them?

Finally, with only three days remaining before their

departure, a telegram from the Danish agent arrived. Maria received it from the delivery boy and looked at it as if it were a mirage that might vanish before her eyes.

"Is that it?" asked Georg from the easy chair where he sat smoking his pipe. He half rose in anticipation.

Maria turned to look at him, her eyes wide, the paper held out gingerly on her palm. "I think so," she whispered. "I'm scared to open it."

Father Wasner stood up from the box of music books that he was packing and reached for it. "Let me read it for you."

Everyone in earshot paused to listen as he slowly opened the envelope and pulled out a thin slip of paper. He cleared his throat and read the message with gusto: "Everything ready for first concert March twelfth Copenhagen."

Immediately the small house erupted in cheers and laughter. "We got it! We got it!" everyone cried. Georg leaned back in his chair and closed his eyes, and Maria bowed her head with her hands clasped in front of her face. "Thank you, precious Jesus," she whispered. "Thank you!"

～

The *Normandie* was a beautiful ship, and the journey across the Atlantic was full of joy and fun and music. Once the family reached Copenhagen, Denmark, the tour went as planned, and their needs were always met, although usually at the last minute.

The family toured Denmark, Norway, Holland, and Sweden. Given Germany's threatening behavior, the Scandinavian people were a bit mistrustful of the von Trapps, but the concerts were still a great success.

During the season, Maria and the girls managed to make a short visit to Salzburg, while Rupert, Werner, Georg, and Father Wasner stayed safely in Italy.

The family was together again, performing in Sweden, when Hitler's army invaded Poland on September 1, 1939. Two days later, Britain and France declared war on Germany. As the borders of all the European nations began to close and foreigners departed for their own countries, the von Trapps' Swedish visas also approached their expiration. Just when the family feared they would have no choice but to return to Austria, tickets arrived from Mr. Wagner for the long voyage back to America.

~

Whereas seeing the Statue of Liberty and the skyscrapers of New York City emerge from the fog for the first time was like an enchanting vision, seeing them for the second time was like coming home and catching sight of an old, dear friend. Standing along the railing of the ship, the von Trapps couldn't stop smiling as the ship inched closer and closer to the harbor. In their excitement they sang a hymn of thanksgiving, delighting everyone nearby.

As soon as the gangplank was lowered, newspaper reporters crowded onto the ship looking for scoops. Of course, when they discovered the presence of the von Trapps and a Norwegian opera singer named Kirsten Flagstad, photographers had to take their pictures for their newspapers.

On the dock, their guide from last season, Mr. Wagner's assistant, stood waiting and waving madly to get their attention. "Welcome home!" he cried jubilantly. "Welcome home, Trapp Family Choir!"

"It's Mr. Snowden!" cried Lorli, pointing and hopping in excitement. Everyone greeted him with joyful cries and hugs. Maria was so relieved to see him that she had to hug him a second time. "How perfectly wonderful to see you again, Mr. Snowden! I feel as if I'm in a happy dream."

She was still elated when she saw the grim-faced immigration officer awaiting them. Every passenger had to be interviewed and approved before he could officially enter the United States, and one by one, the von Trapps presented their visas to the officer. Rupert went first, because he was the only one who had been able to obtain an immigration visa this time. Then it was Father Wasner's turn, then Hedwig's, then Agathe's, and then Maria's.

With a thin-lipped smile that he probably meant as welcoming, the officer scrutinized Maria's face and asked her name and country of origin, as well as several other simple questions. Maria answered calmly and clearly, but she could not stop smiling. She would see the Drinkers again! She would see the Appalachian Mountains again with their stunning autumn colors! She would sing again at the Drinkers' parties!

The officer's next question interrupted her thoughts. "How much time do you intend to spend in America?"

Maria, of course, knew that the answer she was supposed to give was the same amount of time that was specified on her visa: six months. In that moment, though, she was so overcome by the joy of returning to America that she blurted instead, "Oh, I am so glad to be here. I never want to leave again!"

Instantly, the officer's tight friendliness disappeared. His eyes narrowed as he studied her. Then he beckoned to another officer waiting nearby. As the officer approached, he said, "Harold, please escort Mrs. von Trapp and her family to the holding area for further questioning. We may have a problem."

"Oh no, sir!" cried Maria, realizing her mistake. "I didn't mean that I *wouldn't* leave again. I am planning to stay here only six months, as my visa says."

But it was too late. Except for Rupert, because of his special visa, all the von Trapps and Father Wasner were commanded to wait in a separate area until all the passengers had been processed, and then they were all questioned again by another pair of officers. What is your purpose here? Why did you leave Austria? What is your source of income? Who is helping you here? Are you Nazi sympathizers?

Finally, the officers stood up, and the von Trapps and Father Wasner watched them hopefully as they conferred with yet another officer out of their hearing. One of the officers soon returned, this time with a policeman. "We are not yet satisfied with your answers to our questions. Officer Madden here will be keeping an eye on you until we can secure a boat to take you to Ellis Island, where you will stay until we reach an official decision."

"Sir—" began Georg, but the officer was gone. Clearly there would be no discussion about the matter.

For the rest of the day, Father Wasner and the von Trapps—except for Rupert, who had left to seek help —played shuffleboard and gazed through the windows at Brooklyn across the water. At about four o'clock the policeman ordered them to follow him to a motorboat that contained their many pieces of luggage. Despite the fun of riding in a motorboat, the family fell into a worried silence. Except for Lorli and Rosmarie, no one dared to ask what would happen to them, and no one answered the little girls. The adults knew, however, that there would be no restful sleep in the Hotel Wellington tonight, for just ahead was the grim, gray Ellis Island prison, where all foreigners who raised suspicion were sent.

At first the prison was frightening and uncomfortable. It was full of weary travelers from many different nations, and the air was hot and close for October. Despite the warm weather, the heaters were on and the windows were barred shut.

No one explained why they were detained or how long they would be there. They learned that most of the prisoners had been there for several weeks, but some had been there for months! This news worried the von Trapps, for their first concert was in only two weeks. But nothing could be done about it. Here they would remain until the authorities decided to allow them into the United States or to send them back where they came from.

The meals were dreary, and the nights were long and sleepless under undimmed ceiling lights until the officials allowed the lights to be turned off in the women's dormitory so that Johannes could sleep.

Father Wasner was given permission to say Mass, although only for the family, and everyone was allowed outside for a half hour after lunch. The rest of the time the family practiced their music and followed Johannes around, for he had just begun to walk.

Rupert came to visit them on the second day, but he had no good news. On the third day newspaper reporters came to take their photographs for stories about the sad fate of the von Trapps.

The prison wardens were not cruel, and the other

prisoners were friendly and welcomed the singing practices. With the freedom to spend their hours as they wished within the confines of the large holding room, life at the prison was bearable, if not comfortable. All they had to do was wait for their hearing with the authorities. Wait . . . and pray for deliverance.

On the fourth day, a policeman escorted them to the courtroom, where for two and a half hours the family and Father Wasner were questioned by the authorities. Maria was asked the most questions because of her rash comment the day they arrived. Repeatedly, the von Trapps explained who they were and why they had come to America and what they planned to do, but it was no use. The judge still didn't believe them, and he curtly dismissed them from the courtroom.

Solemnly the group returned to the prison cell with the other foreigners and sat down, trying not to cry. Soon Mitzi began to sing, and they all joined in. It was the best way to keep the tears from flowing.

During the second song, an officer poked his head in the room. "Georg von Trapp!" he bellowed.

Immediately Georg jumped up and followed the officer. He returned a few minutes later with a broad grin. "We . . . are . . . *free*!" he cried, throwing his arms wide.

"What?" "How?" "What did they say?" Everyone had questions.

"Well, you will not believe it," said Georg. "The

Drinkers, Mr. Snowden, and Mr. Wagner all contacted their senators and congressmen, insisted we were innocent, and called for our release. Rupert did everything he could, too, of course. And finally the misunderstanding was cleared up!''

It was too wonderful to believe, especially since so many other foreigners had been imprisoned for much longer. Their new friends in the prison shared in their joy with thunderous applause. Then, with a parting gift of two joyous songs, the von Trapps said good-bye and turned their faces toward Brooklyn once more.

The Trapp Family Singers

DR. F. WASNER, CONDUCTOR

SATURDAY NOVEMBER 23

13

THE END OF THE BEGINNING

December 1939

T WELVE THOUSAND DOLLARS," Mr. Wagner said slowly, peering over the rim of his glasses across his large desk at Georg and Maria.

"I don't understand," said Maria. "What does this mean?"

"That's the amount of money I've lost on the Trapp Family Choir this fall."

Georg leaned his elbow on the arm of his chair and stroked his mustache in distress. He and Maria said nothing. Their discouragement was too overwhelming for any words.

"You've sung twenty-four concerts of the forty that I planned," Mr. Wagner continued, "and I just can't give you any more. I can't afford to keep losing money like this."

"But Mr. Wagner, there are no advertisements, no publicity," protested Maria, who remembered the importance of getting their name before the public. "People don't come because they don't know about us. Can we not . . . what do you say? . . . er, spread the word more?"

Mr. Wagner sat back in his chair and folded his hands over his ample belly. Shaking his head, he replied, "I'm sorry, but I hardly see how that will help. The truth is, Captain and Baroness, your family are artists of the highest order. You deserve much better than this. But this is America. I am convinced that American audiences are interested in a different kind of music. In other words, you and America are not made for each other." He waved a hand in their direction. "Go back to Europe, where you will be appreciated for what you are. That is where you will find your lasting success."

Georg and Maria searched for the right words to persuade Mr. Wagner not to give up, to give them more publicity. It had worked last year. Why could it not work this year? Besides, they needed these concerts just as much as they did last year. It was the only way they could earn income to live. With the war in Europe, going back there was the last thing they wanted to do.

Mr. Wagner stood up and held out his hand for them to shake. "I enjoy your choir, I truly do. I will be sorry to see you go, but I know this is for the best. Goodbye, Captain, Baroness. May God bless you all richly and grant you a wonderful future."

Dazed by Mr. Wagner's abrupt cancellation of their season for the second time, Georg and Maria made their way outside and stood still for a moment, watching the bustle of the city street under the cheerful, cloudless sky. Somehow this seemed like an insult. The world had moved on, leaving them with nothing but failure. What now?

Thankfully, the question of housing had already been solved. As Christmas approached, Mr. Drinker had offered them a house that he owned in Merion, Pennsylvania, across from his own beautiful house. It had recently become available, and it was not only furnished but also rent free. All Mr. Drinker wanted in exchange was for the von Trapps to join the musical evenings he often hosted for his fellow music lovers and for Father Wasner to help him translate Bach's cantatas into English from German. It was the perfect arrangement. Still, their final paycheck from Mr. Wagner would soon run out. They couldn't afford to live without doing concerts until their visas expired again.

Troubled and anxious, Georg and Maria made the three-hour journey back to Merion in near silence, both their minds racing. When they had arrived in New York City to meet with Mr. Wagner, they had thought it would be for a business dinner during which they would discuss the details of the second half of the concert season, which was to begin in January. Neither was prepared for his unceremonious cancellation, and they both dreaded explaining to the family what had happened.

Mercifully, no one heard them come in the front door when they arrived, for Johannes was happily banging a pan in the kitchen with a wooden spoon, while Hedwig washed dishes. Slipping up the stairs as quietly as possible, they shut their bedroom door behind them and wearily sat down. In just a few minutes, they would have to gather everyone together to discuss this new turn of events, but right now they couldn't bear to think about it.

"How could we find ourselves in this predicament again?" wondered Georg aloud as he pulled off a shoe. "How could this happen a second time? What are we going to do?"

As discouraged as she was, Maria was starting to feel a little better. Now that they were back among their loved ones and homey comforts, their predicament didn't seem quite so terrible. After all, it was still the Christmas season. Outside it was snowing lightly, and lights shone merrily in every house. Instead of weeping as she might have done otherwise, Maria gazed out the window and thought.

"Do you remember when we met with the bishop back in Salzburg?" she mused. "He said that it was the will of God that we come to America to share our music. Nor was he the only one. Many people have said so, that we bless others by it. Georg, our singing isn't just our job. It isn't just a way of earning money to care for our family. It's our mission. Missions often bring special challenges, but that doesn't mean they must be abandoned. If God calls, one must answer, no matter what, and trust that He will see to the details."

Georg sighed. "Maria, we've done the best we can. What more can we do?"

Putting her shoes in the closet, Maria sat next to Georg on the bed and took his hand. "When God closes a door, somewhere He opens a window. That's what I was always taught, and He's done that for us over and over."

"I think we've opened all the windows by now," replied Georg with a surly grunt. He kicked his other shoe off, sending it flying against the wall.

"I don't think so. I think I see another one. It's a small one, but it may be open."

"What could that possibly be?" asked Georg, looking at her with a weary smile. "What is my wonderful Maria cooking up now?"

Maria didn't answer for a moment. She enjoyed the dramatic effect of letting Georg wait in anticipation. Then she grinned. "Let's look for another manager! We've somehow gotten the idea that Mr. Wagner is our only hope to survive in America, but he isn't the only concert manager around, and he may not even be the best. If he liked us enough to sign us on, maybe someone else will, too."

Georg said nothing, thinking over this possibility.

"Remember how we met several other managers at our Town Hall concert last year? I'd completely forgotten about them because we didn't need a new manager then, but why not contact them? In fact, I remember one manager I really liked. He was warm and friendly and personal. Do you remember him? It was a Mr. Schiff . . . or Schmidt . . . or something like that. Don't you remember?"

"Schang, I believe," said Georg with a decisive nod. "Yes, I do remember. He seemed like a good man. I think he's in New York City, too."

First, though, they needed advice on how to approach a manager, since so far, every manager they had met had approached the von Trapps first. The next morning Maria called Mrs. Pessl, who had been so helpful in getting them publicity last year. Anxious to help in whatever way she could, Mrs. Pessl explained that they needed to set up an audition with Mr. Schang right away. Gathering all her courage, Maria called his office in New York City the next day.

"Columbia Concerts," a woman answered cheerfully. "How may I help you?"

Suddenly, Maria was overcome with shyness. Her English had come a long way in just a year, and she understood it most of the time; however, she still struggled to express her thoughts in English. Georg's mastery of the language was only a little better. Oh, if only she had asked Father Wasner to make the call! Being talented with languages, he was nearly fluent by now. He wasn't nearby, though, so Maria plunged ahead.

"Mr. Schang, please," she said, hoping that would be enough.

"One moment, thank you," said the cheery voice.

With a click, the phone beeped in Maria's ear, and she understood she was on hold. Patiently, she waited, drumming her fingers nervously on the table.

"Yes, this is Mr. Schang," said a gruff, hurried voice.

Maria's heart all but stopped, and her mouth went dry. For a moment she couldn't speak at all. This could be their only chance with Mr. Schang, and she had to explain what she wanted in English! Wait, maybe he knew German. She could at least ask.

"Mr. Schang, do you speak German, please?" she asked as clearly as she could. "This is Baroness von Trapp . . . mother of the Trapp Family Choir. You may know?"

For a moment her introduction was met with silence, and then suddenly he boomed in a jolly tone of welcome, "Baroness von Trapp! How wonderful to hear from you. It has been a very long time, hasn't it? No, I'm afraid I do not speak German, but let's see if I can help you anyway."

Encouraged by his friendliness, Maria relaxed. "I want to ask audition. Will be possible?"

"Well, now," he drawled, "let me see . . . yes, I think so. I would love to hear your family again and discuss the possibilities."

"Oh, thank you much! When is good, please?"

"How about a week from today at ten in the morning?"

"Thank you! Very good, thank you, Mr. Schang," agreed Maria. "Until then!"

When Georg came through the door, Maria told him about the phone call. "Oh Georg," she gushed, "I was so worried, but he couldn't have been nicer. We have one week, so we must rehearse every day, except for maybe Sunday."

Rehearse they did! Everyone—except for Rosmarie and Lorli, who were tasked to keep Johannes out of trouble—was so determined to impress Mr. Schang and win a new contract that they rehearsed all day long. This meant three hours in the morning, three hours after lunch, and three hours after supper every day. They also chose their most difficult, complex pieces, so that Mr. Schang might be all the more impressed. Sometimes Mr. and Mrs. Drinker came to listen and help Father Wasner note any flaws that could be corrected. They never tired of listening to the family sing, especially the pieces by Bach, Mr. Drinker's favorite composer.

At last the big day arrived. Johannes, Lorli, and Rosmarie went to stay with Mr. and Mrs. Drinker for the day, while everyone else took the long train ride to New York City for their audition. They had been instructed to meet Mr. Schang at Steinway Hall. One of his fellow managers, Mr. Coppicus, also came to listen; he had heard the von Trapps sing in Vienna long ago and wanted to hear them again.

As solemnly as they knew how—as was befitting the music of Bach and Palestrina—the Trapp Family Choir sang for a glorious hour. Their voices rang out in bell-like tones as beautiful as ever, and everyone felt as if he was doing his best. Finally, Mr. Schang and Mr. Coppicus rose from their seats and left the auditorium. The von Trapps looked at each other, confused, and waited patiently for whatever came next.

After a few minutes, a young man with a clipboard in his hand entered the hall and approached the family. Maria's heart sank as she saw the apologetic expression on his face.

"Hello, everyone, my name is Frederick Smith. I'm Mr. Schang's assistant. He asked me to thank you for letting him hear your audition, and he says that he and Mr. Coppicus love your music. I also enjoyed your music from just outside the doors. You are truly exquisite.

However . . ." He paused, his eyes shifting downward, as if he was ashamed of his next words. "However, neither he nor Mr. Coppicus will be able to offer you a contract at this time. They don't feel that they can represent you as managers. They are genuinely sorry and appreciate your time and effort in coming to see them."

Silence fell on the hall like a gloomy fog as the von Trapps absorbed this news. No one could think of anything to say. In Maria's mind she saw the last window of opportunity slamming shut, and the small light that had glowed steadily within her was swallowed by darkness. "There is nothing left for us," she thought. "We are done."

Father Wasner was the first to recover his voice, and he stepped forward to thank Mr. Smith with a warm smile. Then Georg and Maria did the same. They returned to the train station in a daze.

"How could it be?" wondered Hedwig aloud, as she gazed glumly out the window. "We sang our hearts out."

Rupert shrugged. "Maybe we should have sung Josquin des Prez instead of Palestrina. That's even more difficult and would have shown better what we could do."

"Or we should have played more on the recorders," suggested Martina. "Mr. Schang seemed to enjoy that."

"I don't think any of those changes would have helped," said Father Wasner, removing his glasses with a sigh and rubbing his eyes. It had been a long week of rehearsals for nothing. As their director, he was as discouraged as the rest of them.

"Why not?" Werner challenged him. "There must have been something we didn't do that we could have done. He clearly likes our music."

Father Wasner shrugged. "I don't know. I just sensed that there were reasons that have nothing to do with the quality of our music. We can always improve, and we've shown that we can perform entire concerts successfully, so I think there was something more that maybe he felt we couldn't—or wouldn't—change."

Agathe crossed her arms and glowered at the trees and meadows rushing past their window. "It doesn't seem fair that he didn't talk to us himself and tell us why. Maybe it's something we could have fixed."

Everyone agreed with solemn nods, except for Maria. She hadn't been listening at all, because in her mind a new window had opened, one she hadn't seen before, and a ray of light was beaming weakly into the darkness. Perhaps if Mr. Schang was willing to hear them once, he would be willing to hear them again, and maybe he would change his mind.

"Next time let's do Bach's—" began Maria.

"What next time? He already said no," interrupted Hedwig, too frustrated to entertain nonsense.

"What do you mean, Mother?" prompted Agathe patiently.

Georg looked at Maria, a faint hope lighting his eyes. He had become used to Maria's ideas by now.

Maria threw up her hands in exasperation. "This family gives up too easily. Where are we? America. It means opportunity! If Mr. Schang took us for one audition, why wouldn't he take us for another?"

"Because he already said no," countered Rupert, a hint of annoyance in his voice.

"Bah!" Maria waved his words away. "We can't afford to give up. We need another manager because we need more concerts. What else can we do but work some more and ask for another audition, and then maybe next time they'll take us!"

"What about auditioning for other managers?" suggested Georg. "Surely these two are not the only ones besides Mr. Wagner."

Maria considered this. It made her feel more hopeful, but she shook her head. "I want Mr. Schang. He is the right man for us. He is kind, friendly, and . . . I just feel good about him. Let's try again with him, and if he still won't take us, we'll find someone else."

So once again, they spent days preparing for a second audition, rehearsing the most difficult pieces they knew and trying to correct the tiniest flaws. Finally, Maria wrote a letter asking for another audition. She didn't dare call again, for fear Mr. Schang would reject the idea without a second thought.

The family waited and prayed for Mr. Schang's reply, which arrived in three days.

"Come anytime," he wrote. "Let us know at least twenty-four hours ahead."

Excited, they set the date with the receptionist at Columbia Concerts. Once again, they made the long journey to New York City for their second audition at Steinway Hall. This time Mr. Schang and Mr. Coppicus were joined by some employees from the office and other people the von Trapps didn't recognize. Maybe these people would help him change his mind.

Unfortunately, as they sang the beautiful, solemn melodies of the Renaissance that they had prepared —an organum, a motet, and a sonata—they saw with dismay that one by one, their listeners began leaving the room, until finally the room was empty. Worried, the family waited again for someone to deliver the final decision. Then Maria alone was called out. And once again, an apologetic assistant firmly told her that the answer was no.

Something in Maria snapped. Hurrying back into the hall to Georg, she asked him to take everyone back to the Hotel Wellington and have lunch in the restaurant. She would be along soon. Then she rushed out of the auditorium again to find the young woman who had delivered the crushing news.

"Please," she said boldly, "I must know. Why Mr. Schang and Mr. Coppicus not want us?"

The young woman, Miss Trumbull, smiled sympathetically and glanced around to see if they were overheard. Then she said to Maria in a low voice, "Your voices and performances are marvelous. There is no question that you are artists in every sense of the word."

"Then why he say no?"

Miss Trumbull looked uncomfortable and looked around the room as if expecting the right words to be painted on the walls. Then she sighed. "It's just that you . . . Baroness . . . don't have any visual appeal. American audiences just won't be attracted enough to your choir to come to your concerts. They won't pay the money required for a ticket."

For a moment Maria looked at her blankly, for she had no idea what "visual appeal" meant. Too embarrassed to ask, she smiled brightly and said, "Thank you much, Miss Trumbull. You are kind."

Maria began the long walk to the Hotel Wellington, where the family was waiting for her, but the words "visual appeal" ran round and round in her head until she finally gave a grunt of exasperation and decided to turn right and walk a few extra blocks to Scribner's bookstore. For a long time, she searched for books on it before she finally gave up. No books had those words on the cover, and the friendly employee who offered to help her couldn't make sense of what she wanted. Finally, she headed back the way she had come and continued toward the hotel.

So deep in thought was she that she was amazed to discover that her feet had taken her not to the hotel at all but to Columbia Concerts! Suddenly a new wave of determination took hold of her, and she hurried to the elevator before she could change her mind. Perhaps she might run into Mr. Schang and just ask him what "visual appeal" meant. Maybe it was something the family could fix!

To her surprise, he was just entering his office from another elevator when she arrived on the fifteenth floor. With a warm, relaxed smile, he ushered her into his office and offered her a seat.

"What can I do for you, Baroness?" he asked kindly. "I'm sorry everything turned out the way it did with your audition this morning."

"Is okay," said Maria with a gallant effort to smile. Then she frowned and shook her head. "No, no, is not okay. Mr. Schang, we show what we can do, and you know we have done many concerts. Why you not take us?"

Heaving a deep sigh, Mr. Schang leaned back in his huge leather chair. "Well, Baroness von Trapp, it has nothing to do with your artistry. You are all true musicians in the best sense of the word. But . . ." He sighed again. "This is difficult for me to say, but you deserve the truth. As good as you are, your program is one of the worst I've ever heard. That piece by Bach was forty-five minutes long! It's beautiful, yes, but only a few classical music lovers will enjoy it. General American audiences won't sit through that. And the recorders are awful, too." He leaned forward on his desk and looked straight into Maria's eyes. "But Baroness, you must understand that by far the worst thing is your family's appearance, especially you women."

"Our appearance?" repeated Maria. "What is that?"

"Well, how you look. Your long dresses with their high necks, the braids down your backs, the clunky shoes like little boys wear, the hair parted in the middle, and your long, solemn faces—so deadly serious! Americans like smiles and laughter and not so many serious songs. Some are fine, of course, but everything you sing . . . it's like attending a funeral! And can't you get some pretty, modern clothes with nylon stockings and high-heeled shoes and put a little rouge on your cheeks and some lipstick on your lips? The men don't need to change anything; they look quite presentable for the most part. It is you women who need a complete change. If you could do that, it would make such a difference. Along with some program changes, of course."

Maria considered his words carefully. The hurt rose within her, threatening to erupt in an angry outburst. At the same time, though, she understood what he meant. Until now, she had never considered that they might look strange to American audiences with their black Austrian *Dirndl* dresses and traditional braids and heavy shoes. Rupert and Werner looked nearly American with their clean-cut, parted haircuts and fine black suits, and Father Werner looked like any other priest with his clerical collar and black shirt and trousers. But she and the girls . . . they were the problem. Or part of it, anyway.

Makeup, though, and showing some of their legs for the sake of an audience? Such immodesty was not to be thought of! Never in her life.

"No," she said firmly. "We can't do that." She paused, wanting to explain but not knowing English well enough to find the words. "A smile, maybe, but . . ."

Mr. Schang was silent. Maria swallowed hard. "Is . . . this . . . last word?" she asked timidly.

"I'm afraid so, Baroness von Trapp. I'm truly sorry."

It didn't seem right to Maria. She hadn't lived in America for long, but she knew that in this country people could say what they wanted, live and worship the way they wanted, and wear what they wanted. Suddenly, she felt both exhausted from the efforts of the last three weeks and angry at Mr. Schang's harsh judgment. With a great huff, she grabbed a large book sitting at the corner of his desk, lifted it up, and slammed it down.

"I thinked America a *free* country. Is *not*!" With that, Maria rose and haughtily walked out. Only when she reached the elevator did she let her tears begin to fall. It was all too much!

"Excuse me. Baroness von Trapp?" a pleasant voice asked behind her. It was Mr. Schang's assistant.

Wiping her eyes quickly, Maria turned and tried to

smile. After all, what had happened wasn't the kind young woman's fault. "Yes, Miss Trumbull?"

"Mr. Schang would like to see you again in his office, if you wouldn't mind."

Maria was bewildered and reluctant to hear any more criticism from Mr. Schang, but she turned and followed the young woman. In Mr. Schang's doorway she stood stiffly and glowered at him. "You want me?"

"Yes, Baroness, please sit down again," Mr. Schang said, beckoning to the chair. In his eyes was a look of defeat.

"I will stand," said Maria stubbornly.

He sighed and stood up instead. "I've changed my mind. Maybe you will make it in America all right with the clothes you are wearing. I'd like to try it for a year and find out."

Maria's eyes widened in delight.

"But," he added quickly, "you will need a lot of publicity and advertising, which is expensive. Could you spend maybe five thousand of your own money on the publicity? You will almost certainly earn it back over time."

Maria thought of the $250 they had in the bank. How on earth would they get another $4,750? But out loud she said, "Will try," and shook his hand. "Thank you for chance, Mr. Schang. Very much."

That evening back at home, as Maria told the events of the day to the family and the Drinkers, who had come to visit, everyone was excited until she confessed her promise to provide $5,000 for the advance publicity. To her astonishment, Mr. Drinker immediately offered to loan them half of the money if they could find someone else to provide the other half. Within fifteen minutes, Maria had called a woman in New York who had once offered her help, and the miracle was complete. They had the $5,000 they needed to begin.

Once more Maria took the long train ride to New York City with Georg to deliver the two checks to Mr. Schang. "Here you go, Mr. Schang. We borrowed for the year." She clasped his hand in hers and smiled into his eyes. "You not regret—never!"

His smile broadly stretching from ear to ear, Mr. Schang bellowed, "Well, congratulations! Let's get started right away. We have no time to lose, since it's so late in the season. But to begin, we must take care of the most important things to turn your artistry into concerts that everyone will want to attend—and so that you and I can earn our much-needed profits."

"Most important things? What is that?" asked Georg.

"Well, your name, for starters," replied Mr. Schang. Grabbing a piece of paper and a pen from his desk, he dashed off a few words. "Up until now, you have been the Trapp Family Choir, but that sounds too churchy. Many people will not find that appealing, so we must change your name. From now on you are"—he held up the paper triumphantly, so that Georg and Maria could read what he had written—"the Trapp Family Singers!"

14

HOME SWEET AMERICAN HOME

April 1942

O NE SUNNY SPRING AFTERNOON, as the family bus approached Merion after a long, successful tour in the Midwest, the von Trapps agreed that Mr. Schang was the best thing that had ever happened to them. With his help, Father Wasner's direction, and the Drinkers' unfailing support, not to mention visa extensions from the U.S. government due to war conditions, the family of singers had been transformed and back on tour.

Although they kept their Austrian folk wear, they learned to brighten their appearance with smiles and a touch of makeup. Outspoken Maria also began talking to the audience, sometimes telling stories to make them laugh. Father Wasner added some beloved American folk songs to the program of mostly classical music.

People flocked to their concerts all over the country, and within five seasons the von Trapps were known everywhere. Maria and Georg's main sorrow was that Johannes had to be left behind with a nanny during their tours, at least until he was old enough to join in the singing. Lorli and Rosmarie, however, had left behind their boarding school to be homeschooled on the bus.

With joy and gratitude in their hearts the family burst into song.

> Triumph, all ye cherubim!
> Sing with us, ye seraphim!
> Heav'n and earth resound the hymn:
> Salve, salve, salve, Regina!

"Bravo! Bravo!" cried Rudi the bus driver, pounding the steering wheel of the big blue bus to applaud the singing. "That was magnificent! Always my favorite hymn, and you just lift my soul the way you sing it. Thank you for indulging me one more time."

"You are most welcome," said Georg, reaching over from his seat to pat the driver on the shoulder. "We wish we could do much more to show you how much we appreciate your faithful service to us this season. Perhaps we can take you out to dinner some evening when we are in New York?"

"That would be marvelous, Captain," replied Rudi.

"That was the perfect song to end our season with, Papa. What a tour this has been!" cried Martina from the back row.

Georg nodded. "It certainly has."

"I think you have the entire Midwest in your back pocket!" cried Rudi gleefully.

Maria frowned. "In our back . . . what does that mean?"

He waved at her in apology. "Oh, I'm sorry, Baroness. That just means that everyone loved your concerts. I'm sure they'll welcome you back anytime."

"Oh, that's good to know," Maria said, still baffled by the strange idiom.

"Papa, are we almost there yet?" called ten-year-old Lorli from the cot in the back of the bus. She had a headache from banging her head on the door of the restaurant where they had eaten lunch and was lying down.

"Only about a half hour more!" called Rudi. "Soon you'll be home."

"Only a half hour more before we can see Johannes again," said Maria wistfully. "Do you think he's been happy with Martha at home?"

Georg smiled sympathetically at her and patted her arm. "Now, now, Maria, you always worry too much. He's been just fine."

Then he stood up and faced the family. "Actually, this is a good time for us to discuss something important. I think we have just enough time before we get home. Can everyone hear me?"

Eleven faces turned up to him, and the lively chattering hushed.

"Mother and I have been discussing this privately, and now it's time to hear your thoughts." Georg paused, trying hard to suppress the pride he felt about what he was about to say but finding it difficult. A grin spread slowly across his face, and then he chuckled.

"What's so funny, Papa?" asked Werner.

"Well, I was going to pretend that we were bankrupt again and give you all a big scare for a joke, but I just can't do it," confessed Georg. He took a breath as everyone laughed and then continued. "The fact is that we have some very exciting news. We were just examining our bank account and talking to Mr. Schang the other day. For the first time since arriving in America, we are debt free. Every cent has been paid off . . . and we have a nice sum saved up in the bank."

The bus erupted in cheers and applause. Georg held up his hand to silence them. "And that's not all. Because we have done so well these past few seasons, we can think about having a real vacation this year!"

More cheers and applause erupted, and this time Rupert and Werner stomped their feet as hard as they could to add to the din.

"Where are we going?" asked Mitzi.

Georg shrugged. "I'm open to ideas. Where would you all like to go? Let's listen to everyone and then pray about what to do."

Everyone had ideas. Maria wanted to return to the wide-open skies of New Mexico, Father Wasner wanted to see the hills of Kentucky again, Rupert and Werner wanted to climb in the Rocky Mountains, and the girls were divided between Cape Cod and the tropical beaches of Florida. Georg wanted to go to the seashore, too, though where exactly he didn't much care. It was hard to come to an agreement.

Finally, Georg said, "Let's put that decision aside temporarily. We will talk about it again in two weeks."

"Why two weeks?" asked Johanna, who liked to take immediate action whenever someone had an exciting idea.

Georg grinned again. This was the best part of the news he had to share, as far as he was concerned. "Well, a couple of days ago, I was talking to Mr. Schang on the telephone about our transportation costs for next season, and he told me that we would save money by driving our own cars instead of commissioning the bus." He paused for effect, enjoying the family's breathless anticipation. "So, tomorrow, after we've all unpacked, Mother and I are going to go shopping for a car!"

Maria held up two fingers. "We'll need two, Georg."

"Right, *two* cars. From now on we can go any-where!"

"But I will miss you all next fall!" shouted Rudi, who already knew about the plan.

Everyone started clapping and cheering again, but once more Georg held up his hand for silence. "Hold on, that's not all!"

"There's *more*?" Agathe said in amazement.

"We will indeed find somewhere nice to go for the summer, but as soon as I get a driver's license—and Rupert and Werner, you'll need to, as well, and per-haps Mother—"

"Oh Georg, not *me*!" exclaimed Maria, aghast at the idea. "All that traffic, and it's so fast! No, you and the boys go right ahead. Maybe Father Wasner should, too."

"Anyway," continued Georg, who was anxious to reveal the rest of his news, "after we get our cars and licenses, we are going to spend two wonderful, quiet weeks in New Jersey at the Drinkers' cabin. They have offered it to us free of charge. It's in the woods near a creek."

"And then we'll decide about the summer after we come back?" asked Hedwig.

Georg nodded. "That's right—or maybe we'll de-cide while we're there. What do you all think?"

After the long touring season with nearly a hundred concerts, everyone agreed that the new plan sounded perfect. They were exhausted and ready for a long rest, and they missed three-year-old Johannes. It was time for the family to be complete again.

Within a week Georg and Maria had found two used cars in good condition that they could afford—a Lincoln Continental and a Cadillac—and it wasn't long before the necessary driver's licenses were obtained. Georg, Rupert, and Werner already knew how to drive because the family had owned a car in Salzburg; they needed to learn only the laws for driving in the United States. Before they knew it, the family and Father Wasner were off to New Jersey for two relaxing weeks at the Drinkers' cabin.

At the end of May, they returned home refreshed and ready for new plans. It was time to decide once and for all where to spend the summer. Surprisingly, though, the answer came to them in a letter the very day they returned.

"Mother and I have finally decided where we'll spend the rest of the summer," Georg said as the family gathered for the rosary after dinner. In his hand he waved a letter. "A very kindhearted man who saw our last concert heard that we were looking for a place. He just wrote to us offering a cottage he owns . . . well, not really a cottage, more like a tourist home for travelers. Its name is the Stowe-Away, and it houses twenty people. I thought it sounded just right for us."

"Where is it?" asked Father Wasner.

"Vermont," replied Georg. "High in the mountains

above a little village called Stowe. Mother and I would like to accept his offer, because the price is manageable and we have been longing for a cooler summer."

"It sounds relaxing and quiet," suggested Rosmarie agreeably.

"I think it will be very quiet," said Georg. "He says that the village has a small grocery store, a gas station, and some other businesses. We can go on hikes as we used to and enjoy the serenity. After all the noise and travel of this past season, it will be good for us."

The living room was quiet for a moment as everyone thought about the places the family had discussed earlier. The seashore, the Rockies, and New Mexico sounded much more exciting than the mountains of Vermont. On the other hand, it would be something new. Although they had once sung a concert in Vermont, it had been near the southern border, so they hadn't seen much of the state. Why not give it a try?

Over the next week, Maria made the necessary arrangements with the house's owner; then they packed up the cars and headed north. Only Georg was apprehensive as he led the caravan along the highways of Pennsylvania and into New York. He knew little about Vermont. He had heard only that it was mountainous and cold and had nothing interesting to see. It sounded a little grim, he thought. Perhaps the mountains were so far north that they had little foliage. What if it were just rocky barrens?

Sighing in frustration, he reflected that he should

have spent more money to take the family somewhere with interesting things to do, as they did in Austria. How they had all missed their hiking, camping, and biking trips, as well as the occasional concerts in Salzburg during these past few years! Merion was just a residential suburb, and New York City grew wearisome after a while with all its chaos and bustle. Their touring and rehearsals had left them with little opportunity to explore other parts of the country from beyond the windows of the bus.

The family deserved more than just an isolated house in the mountains, Georg told himself. It wouldn't be much of a summer vacation if they were miserable with boredom. Well, he reasoned, at least they could do some hiking, and maybe they could take a day or two to drive to the coast for a day at the beach. It would be chilly water so far north, but he had heard there were some nice beaches in Maine.

As they sped farther and farther north, the Appalachians grew into lush, green mountains that took the family's breath away with their beauty. Quaint towns met them along the way with their neat village greens and saltbox houses, and every so often a towering white steeple would point to God over the treetops.

"Why, this is beautiful!" cried Maria in amazement as the vistas from the highway began to spread over the tops of the mountain ranges.

"It reminds me of Austria," said Agathe approvingly.

She had struggled with homesickness from time to time, and the familiar scenery was comforting.

Finally, late in the afternoon, they arrived in the little village of Stowe. Georg and Rupert stopped at the gas station to fill up the cars. The others got out to stretch their legs and to walk down the road a bit.

"What a charming town!" said Martina. "I think I'll like staying here. I wonder if the house is close by."

It hardly mattered where the house was at this point, for everyone was optimistic that they would like it wherever it was. And they did. The large white farmhouse, just three miles out of town, was neat and well maintained with lots of sunny, cheerful rooms that were well appointed with everything guests would need. Instead of looking into the windows of the houses next door, now they looked to the daisy-filled meadow across the road or the mountaintops in the distance. After a couple of days, it seemed somehow that they could breathe again. Georg said a prayer of thanks to God for providing them with such a wonderful place, despite his worries.

The woods and pastures and nearby swimming holes became the von Trapps' playground for the next two months. They hiked and swam and rested and played games, and once they took turns with a couple of bicycles their neighbors had offered them for the day. It was a wonderful, beautiful, glorious summer.

One day, a friend stopped to visit on his way from

Canada back to his home in Massachusetts. He, too, had been a refugee. He was from Germany and had arrived a couple of years earlier than the von Trapps, barely escaping Hitler's iron fist.

"This is perfectly delightful," he said as Georg and Maria entertained him in the living room that evening with coffee and *Apfelstrudel*, which was still Maria's favorite dessert. "How did you come to find such an idyllic place to spend the summer?"

Maria explained how it had all happened, and then Georg added, "We're having a hard time getting used to the fact that we have to go back to Philadelphia. The crowds, the traffic . . ." He trailed off and sighed. "We have dear friends in Merion, but this place . . . it reminds us of Austria. We have missed the Alps so much."

Their friend stared at them in consternation. "Well," he said, "what's making you go back? Other than your season touring, you have no reason to go anywhere else. Just buy something here in Vermont."

Georg laughed and shook his head. "Impossible," he said, puffing on his pipe. "We have some savings now but not nearly enough to buy a house."

"But, but, but . . . ," his friend spluttered, "you don't need to have all the money in your pocket to buy a house in America."

"You don't?" asked Georg. This was strange news. "Houses surely aren't free!"

"No, no," his friend chuckled, "but you can pay

little by little. Just pay some now and then get what is called a mortgage. Every month you pay some of the cost of the house until it's paid off! That's how most Americans buy their houses."

Maria and Georg were silent, thinking. Could this be true? Did they truly have the chance to own a house in America, after all, and in these wonderful mountains? Up to this moment, they had assumed that they would need to save for many years before they could buy a place of their own, no matter what country they lived in, but now . . . it seemed too good to be true!

After their friend left the next morning, Maria and Georg talked a long time about the possibilities. They did have some money in the bank now, but they also had a difficult decision to make. The family needed new wardrobes. For several months Maria had been planning a huge shopping trip for everyone. They had been wearing Austrian clothes since they had arrived in America, and Hedwig had even enlisted everyone's help to make some new ones of lighter fabric. These clothes still had some wear left, but now that the government had determined that they could stay in America as refugees and pursue citizenship, it seemed fitting to get new American clothes to help them fit into society. The problem was, they couldn't buy proper wardrobes for eleven people and also buy a house.

Back and forth the family went, trying to decide which was more important, but finally it was decided. They would buy a house. And not just any house! They would buy a farm, where they could raise their own dairy cows and grow vegetables and have an orchard and any number of things to help them be self-sufficient during the months they were not touring around the United States. Everyone was beginning to feel tired of the constant traveling and wished for a permanent residence that they didn't have to leave for such long stretches at a time, but right now, touring was still the best source of income.

Up and down and across the state of Vermont they roamed for the rest of the summer, searching for a farm to call their own. With so little money to spend on a down payment, though, they couldn't find anything in good-enough condition to buy. At last came a Saturday when they had to stop searching and give a performance. This time it was at a nearby U.S. Army camp. The commander had heard they were in the area and asked for a short concert.

The evening concert went beautifully—so well, in fact, that the commander asked if they would return the next Sunday to sing Mass for the Catholic soldiers with Father Wasner presiding. On Wednesday the von Trapps would have to leave Stowe to return to Merion, so it seemed a beautiful finish to their happy summer.

After singing Bach at the morning Mass under the cloudless blue sky, the family said good-bye to the soldiers and started the four-mile journey back to the house. Suddenly, Georg slowed the car and pointed up a sunny slope just in front of them.

"A place like that—that's where I'd be happy to spend the rest of my days," he wistfully said to Maria.

Quietly they gazed at the slope, awash in sunshine and wildflowers. It was the first place Georg had ever seen that reminded him so much of his homeland. With a sigh of regret, he continued on, with a yearning he could never fully express.

As much as he cherished their dear friends the Drinkers and Professor Albrecht back in Merion, he didn't want to leave and return to the busyness of the city. Nor, he knew, did Maria. But it couldn't be helped. They had tried to find something to buy in Vermont and just couldn't. Maybe after this next season they could try again—or perhaps they might find something in New Hampshire or Maine.

The next morning, as the family finished breakfast, a knock came at the front door. Werner opened it to a kind-looking man holding his hat. He held out his hand and said, "Good morning! My name is Benjamin Allen, and I heard that you want to buy a farm. I want to sell mine. Would you like to come have a look at it today?"

Five days later, unbelievably, the sunny slope Georg had longed for on the drive home from the camp was theirs, for on it was the very farm the man had offered them at a price they could afford. It had a large house in fair condition and several outbuildings. The meadows and mountain vista filled their souls with joy. It seemed too good to be true, but by Thursday it was theirs!

After everyone gathered at the town clerk's office to watch Georg, Maria, and Mr. Allen sign the deed, Georg went straight to the village hardware store and bought an ax and a box of nails. Then they returned to the farm and began making plans, while Rupert and Werner went to work cutting down two small trees in their—their!—woods. Together they made a cross twelve feet high and carried it to the highest point on their property. As they climbed the hill, Father Wasner led the rest of the family in a procession behind them, filling the warm afternoon with songs of thanksgiving and praise to God for this unexpected, bountiful blessing.

For several days they worked to set up the house with basic necessities, so that it would be ready for them when they returned from Merion with all their possessions. When everything was ready, they had to hurry back to Pennsylvania. They still had much to do before they could live on the farm, and everyone had to help. The rental house in Merion had to be cleaned and closed up, and they had to rehearse for their new tour, which was to begin in September. All their plans for the farm would have to wait a little while, but soon they would return to stay.

~

The October sun was setting in brilliant hues of purple, rose, and gold when Georg and Maria finally laid aside their work gloves and set out for an evening stroll. In Merion they had needed to walk along sidewalks if they wanted fresh air, but here on their new farm they could walk anywhere. Tonight they chose the meadow, which overlooked a valley and offered a view of nine mountains in the distance. In different lights the mountains took on an array of colors—gray, green, blue—but tonight they were on fire as the setting sun touched the autumn forests.

"Look at that," said Maria, stopping to gaze at the view in awe. "Look, Georg. I can't believe this land is ours. It's like a dream."

Georg lit his pipe and took a contented puff. "I must say that in some ways I feel richer here than I ever did back in Austria, when I had mansions and servants. It's funny how one's perspective can change."

"Do you still miss Austria?" asked Maria, slipping her arm into his and drawing close. The breeze picked up loose tendrils of her hair and blew them across her face. She closed her eyes, reveling in the cool, fragrant air and the peace that wrapped around her like a soft blanket.

"Of course," said Georg frankly. "I'll always be an Austrian. I'll always miss my homeland. But I do love this farm, and America is a good place for us. I have no complaints."

Maria nodded in agreement.

"Look at that!" said a voice. Maria and Georg turned to see Father Wasner approaching them.

Maria smiled. "Yes, Father, we were just talking about the view. It's so beautiful."

"I'm not interrupting you, am I?" the priest asked, suddenly realizing that the couple might want privacy. "I was just taking an evening walk and didn't realize you were here until I was nearly upon you. My mind is on many things, making plans and praying."

"Oh no, Father Wasner," said Maria. "You aren't intruding at all. Surely you aren't thinking of leaving us, are you? I hope that isn't what you're planning."

Father Wasner stood next to them, taking in the sunset with a deep sigh of contentment. "No, I couldn't leave this beautiful mountain yet. Maybe someday God will lead me elsewhere, but for now, I plan to see the Trapp Family Singers through as many seasons as they'll have me."

Maria breathed a sigh of relief. "That's good to hear. You're like family to us now. We can hardly imagine life without you."

The three were silent for a moment, thinking. Then Maria said quietly, "But Father, I have a sin I need to confess, and I didn't realize it until now."

"Of course. Why don't we go somewhere more private?" invited Father Wasner, gesturing with his arm away from Georg.

"No, somehow I think Georg and I are united on this one."

Georg took another puff of his pipe and waited. In his heart he knew what she would say.

"What is it, Maria?" asked Father Wasner with an encouraging smile.

"In all these years since leaving Austria," said Maria slowly, "I have never really trusted God to provide one of the most important things we needed. I despaired of ever having it again."

"And what is that?"

"All of this!" said Maria, embracing the world around them with one sweep of her arm.

"A home," said Georg.

EPILOGUE

February 1973

"J UDY, THAT WAS A WONDERFUL BREAKFAST, as always," Maria said to the restaurant chef. "Are you sure you weren't born in Austria?"

The plump cook burst into laughter. "Oh, Mrs. von Trapp, you are a hoot. Do I sound like I was born in Austria? But thank you for the compliment."

The dining room was extra noisy this morning, for six inches of snow had fallen during the night at the Trapp Family Lodge, and everyone was trying to get outside for cross-country skiing. Maria hoped that the grounds were ready. She knew that Werner and Johannes had been out early, working to prepare for the many skiers that would soon spread across the mountainsides.

It looked as if the children and Father Wasner were already busy with the guests, too. Hedwig and Mitzi stood near a window, deep in conversation with another young woman about their age, and Johanna served coffee to an elderly couple. Maria sighed with satisfaction. The dining room was warm and fragrant with cinnamon and coffee, and all their guests seemed excited for the day ahead. Outside, the snow still fell softly, but the forecast predicted some clearing later on. It would be a perfect day at the lodge, just the way she liked it.

She needed to be on her way to the gift shop, which was a half mile down the road. A new shipment of *The Sound of Music* memorabilia had arrived yesterday, and she knew everyone would be flooding the gift shop to buy those items today. The movie's first revival had just opened in Burlington, and it was one reason for some of the heavy ski traffic this weekend. Everyone wanted to meet the family that had inspired the Oscar-winning musical, even if it wasn't an accurate portrayal of the von Trapps' story.

After she put on her parka and boots, Maria made her way to the front door, momentarily stopping to press her hand to Georg's portrait, which hung in a prominent place nearby. It had been more than twenty-five years since his death in 1947, but she still missed him. He was still one of the greatest men she had ever known.

"Ready, Mother?" asked Rupert, who was dressed for the short drive in a fur-lined cap, heavy gloves, and a down parka. He held her arm as they made their way to the Jeep. Maria had had her license now for many years, but she still didn't like to drive in heavy snow, so Rupert always took her on days like this.

She smiled as the vehicle passed a young family in ski suits. They were heading for the bunny slope with their toddler. It must be his first time, she mused.

"It's been such a long time since I skied, Rupert," she said. "I should really get back to it if I'm going to run a ski lodge."

Rupert steered carefully around a mound of snow in the road. "Sure, that would be a great idea. I'll help you if you want."

"You'd just laugh at me," she predicted, imagining herself falling and rolling down a slope.

He grinned. "Probably," he admitted, "but you'd be an expert again in no time. You want me to take you into Burlington and help you choose some skis?"

"Well, I'll think about it. Drop me off right here, will you, please?" she said, pointing to the entrance of the gift shop's driveway. "There's a hat in the snow. I should probably put it in the lost and found. Besides, you might get stuck in the driveway."

Rupert brought the Jeep to a stop. "Okay, Mother, I'll be back to pick you up about noon."

Maria picked up the hat—a child's, it seemed—and trudged carefully down the plowed walk. It was bitterly cold, but a deep thrill fluttered in her chest anyway. Something about the day was exquisitely beautiful, almost transcendent. She stopped, just to smell the clean mountain air and feel the petal-like flakes drop gently onto her upturned cheeks. Taking a deep breath, she turned slowly in a circle, feasting her eyes on the mountains that rippled all around the property, dipping into valleys that had become ski country for the winter and then climbing, climbing, climbing up to the heavens, as if reaching for God. Raising her arms briefly in thanksgiving, she continued down the path to the front door.

In the quiet shop, she set her briefcase down and turned on the lights and the thermostat. There were the several brown boxes ready for unpacking, and her watch told her she had an hour before she opened the store, plenty of time to fill the shelves.

When she was finished, she prepared the cash register for the day and turned the sign to OPEN. Sitting down on her stool, she opened her briefcase and pulled out the pile of fan mail that had come yesterday. She, Rosmarie, and Lorli tried hard to keep up with the many letters people wrote to the family since *The Sound of Music* premiered in 1965.

After more than twenty years of touring not only the United States but also Europe, Australia, and South America, the family had stopped performing in 1955 to focus on other things. At first they had looked forward with relief to a quiet, ordinary life just working their farm, but the Broadway musical and the recent movie, their multiseason music camp, and the new ski lodge had changed all that. Now the von Trapps were the most famous family in America.

Maria opened letter after letter, smiling as she always did at the lovely praise and kind words people wanted to share—some about the movie, some about their concert memories, and some about their memorable visits to the Trapp Family Lodge. Finally, she came to the last envelope in the pile and slit it open. As she read, her eyes began to fill with tears.

"Dear Mrs. von Trapp," it began.

> My name is Angela, and I am eighteen years old. I live near Chicago, but last summer I had the privilege of spending a weekend at the Trapp Family Lodge and meeting you briefly in the dining room. It was a wonderful experience, and I want to thank you for that. I've also bought all your albums, and I've listened to them over and over. They have blessed me so much!
>
> I am hoping you can help me. I am in my first year of college, but I am sensing a call to become a nun in an order that serves the poor. I love God with all my

heart and am a faithful Catholic, but the idea scares me. Recently, I heard you give a talk at a church near my hometown, and I so appreciated everything you had to say. One thing you said really stuck with me: "The important thing in life is to find out the will of God and then to go and do it." I am afraid that if I surrender my life to Him like that, I will regret it. I am used to being independent, and I'm afraid to trust Him. Mrs. von Trapp, do you ever regret leaving behind your dreams and following the path that became your life? Is it worth following the will of God? I hope you have time to answer me, but if not, I understand. Thank you for listening!

Maria put down the letter and pulled a pen and a pad of paper from a drawer. She smiled to herself and let her mind drift back to the past, far away across the ocean to the elegant Villa Trapp. This letter would be a pleasure to write.

BUT WHAT ABOUT . . . ?

The von Trapps' adventures didn't stop with the purchase of their Vermont farm. Far from it! In fact, the family continued to tour until 1955, becoming so famous that they were soon performing all over the world. They recorded many record albums, too. And singing wasn't all the family became known for, either.

GEORG—A decorated war hero and beloved father and husband, Captain Georg von Trapp died of lung cancer at age sixty-seven on May 30, 1947. He was buried in the family cemetery on the grounds of the Trapp Family Lodge. He never returned to Austria. With Maria and the children, he started the Trapp Family Music Camp at the old Civilian Conservation Corps camp where the family performed just before purchasing their farm in Stowe, Vermont. He also founded Trapp Family Austrian Relief with Maria in January 1947, serving as president until his death.

MARIA—Seemingly tireless, Maria possessed an energy and a strong personality that kept her involved with many activities after buying the Stowe farm with Georg. She was instrumental in establishing the Trapp Family Music Camp and Trapp Family Austrian Relief, as well as in developing the farm into the tourist destination that it is today. She continued touring with the family after Georg's death until the group stopped giving concerts in 1955. When *The Sound of Music* opened on Broadway, she helped prepare actress Mary Martin to portray her on stage, and she attended the gala performance.

In 1956 she went to the South Sea Islands with Maria, Rosmarie, Johannes, and Father Wasner in the hope of founding a missionary training center. Although this plan was never fulfilled, she stayed busy afterward. She traveled to Austria to stock the Trapp Family Lodge gift shop and gave lectures throughout the United States. She also wrote several books, including *The Story of the Trapp Family Singers*; *Maria: My Own Story*; *Yesterday, Today, and Forever*; *The Trapp Family Book of Christmas Songs*; *Around the Year with the Trapp Family*; *When the King Was Carpenter*; and *A Family on Wheels: Further Adventures of the Trapp Family Singers*. Maria died of heart failure at age eighty-two on March 28, 1987, and is buried with other family members in the family cemetery at the Trapp Family Lodge.

FATHER FRANZ WASNER—After faithfully directing the von Trapps for their entire career, as well as living with them as both a close friend and a spiritual leader, Father Wasner traveled to the South Seas with Maria and several of the children in 1956. He decided to stay in Fiji, where he served in missions for five years. After his service ended, he was sent to the Holy Land, where he directed a papal mission, and then he served as the rector of a seminary in Rome. He retired to Salzburg, where he died on June 21, 1992, at eighty-six years old.

RUPERT ("Friedrich" in the musical)—After settling in Stowe, the oldest von Trapp child was called into military service for the United States during World War II. After he returned, he became an American citizen in 1948. He married in that same year and continued to tour with the family. Eventually, he pursued his medical degree in the United States and set up a successful practice in Rhode Island. He became the father of six children. When he retired, he moved back to Vermont and died at the Trapp Family Lodge on February 22, 1992, at the age of eighty. Rupert is buried in the family cemetery there.

AGATHE ("Liesl" in the musical)—Becoming an American citizen in 1948, the oldest von Trapp daughter continued to tour with the family and help run the Trapp Family Music Camp and Trapp Family Lodge until after the last concert was performed in Concord, New Hampshire, in 1955. She never married. She left the Trapp Family Lodge in 1956 to start a kindergarten with her friend Mary Lou Kane. Together they ran their kindergarten first in Stowe and then in Baltimore, Maryland, until 1993. After she retired in the Baltimore suburbs, Agathe began pursuing other talents—drawing and painting. She held several exhibits, including one at the Austrian Embassy in Washington, D.C., and sold many of her paintings. She illustrated *The Trapp Family Book of Christmas Songs* and her own autobiography, *Memories Before and After* The Sound of Music. Agathe died in Baltimore of heart failure at age ninety-seven on December 28, 2010, and she is buried in the family cemetery at the Trapp Family Lodge.

MARIA (Mitzi) ("Louisa" in the musical)—After singing with the Trapp Family Singers until 1955, Maria decided that her true life's work was in missions. She spent the next thirty-two years as a missionary, traveling around the world and working especially in Papua New Guinea. When she retired in 1987, she returned to Vermont and lived in a small cottage on the family property. She played the accordion, taught Austrian folk dancing with Rosmarie, and often served as hostess for the lodge guests. She died at home of natural causes at age ninety-nine on February 18, 2014, and is buried in the family cemetery at the Trapp Family Lodge.

WERNER ("Kurt" in the musical)—Like Rupert, Werner served in the U.S. Army during World War II. Upon his return home in 1948, he became a U.S. citizen and built a stone chapel at the farm in gratitude to God. He fell in love with Erika, a childhood friend of Martina's, during her 1948 visit from Austria.

They married just before her visa expired that same year, and they had six children.

Werner continued to tour with the Trapp Family Singers until the last concert, and he helped found a music school in Pennsylvania. Eventually, he bought a dairy farm in Waitsfield, Vermont, which he operated until his retirement. During the years that followed, he returned to artistic pursuits, such as carpet weaving and organ playing. He died at age ninety-one on October 11, 2007, in Waitsfield and is buried in the family cemetery at the Trapp Family Lodge.

HEDWIG ("Brigitta" in the musical)—Like her older siblings, Hedwig became a citizen in 1948 and continued to tour with the family until the choir disbanded in 1955. After remaining at the lodge for a short time, she became a teacher. First she taught in Hawaii, and then she returned to Austria to teach in the Tyrol region. Upon her return to Vermont, Hedwig's asthma became so severe that she spent her final years in Austria at Zell am See. She lived with her mother's youngest sister, Tante Joan, whose home was next to the Erlhof, where Hedwig was born. There Hedwig lived peacefully until asthma claimed her life on September 14, 1972. She was fifty-five. She is buried in the family cemetery at the Trapp Family Lodge.

JOHANNA ("Marta" in the musical)—Along with her older siblings, Johanna became a citizen in 1948 and then left the Trapp Family Singers to marry her fiancé, Ernst Winter, who had roots in Vienna. The couple moved permanently back to Austria, where they fulfilled Johanna's dream of a large family by having seven children. Johanna was also an artist who worked with watercolor, clay, and ceramics. Upon her death at age seventy-five on November 25, 1994, her watercolors were honored with an exhibition in Salzburg. She is buried in Vienna, Austria.

MARTINA ("Gretl" in the musical)—Sadly, the youngest of the original seven von Trapp children did not live to see the final concert season of 1955. She became a citizen in 1948 with the rest of the family and then in 1949 married a French Canadian, Jean Dupiere, whom she met at the Trapp Family Music Camp. When she became pregnant a couple of years later, she decided to skip the 1951 concert season to stay in Vermont and prepare for motherhood. Complications arose during the delivery, and both she and the baby died on February 25, 1951. Martina was thirty years old and is buried in the family cemetery at the Trapp Family Lodge.

ROSMARIE—Extremely shy, the oldest of Maria's biological children suffered badly from stage fright and didn't like performing with the Trapp Family Singers, so she left the group before it disbanded. In 1948 she became a citizen with the rest of the family. From 1956 to 1959 she worked as a missionary in Papua New Guinea, after which she joined the Community of the Crucified One, which had a branch in Vermont. Around 1968 she had a spiritual awakening in which her faith in God was renewed after years of struggle. As her mother's health failed, she nursed her until her death in 1987. After Maria's death, Rosmarie began spending part of each year in Vermont giving guests of the Trapp Family Lodge recorder lessons and conducting sing-alongs. The other part of the year she spent in a community near Jerusalem. As of 2021, she lives in Stowe near the lodge and is in excellent health.

ELEONORE (Lorli)—The middle child of Georg and Maria, Lorli became a citizen and toured with the family until the choir disbanded in 1955. Just before the touring ended, she married Hugh Campbell in 1954; they had met at the Trapp Family Music Camp. The couple settled near the family farm in Waitsfield, where Werner also settled. Along with raising seven daughters, she enjoyed gardening, sewing, and cooking, and she was active with groups promoting traditional family values. As of 2021, she lives in an assisted living home in Vermont.

JOHANNES—The only von Trapp born in the United States, Johannes is the most business-minded member of the family and the most like Maria in temperament. He joined the Trapp Family Singers at age nine and continued singing with the group until it disbanded. As an adult he attended both Dartmouth and Yale and earned a master's degree in forestry. This gave him the knowledge he needed to design, build, and manage the ski trails at the Trapp Family Lodge, which made it America's first cross-country ski resort. When the lodge began to struggle financially, he took over the business and is today president of the Trapp Family Corporation. He met his wife, Lynne, when she came to work at the lodge in 1967, and they married in the family chapel two years later. The couple have two children, Sam and Kristina, who own and operate the lodge with their spouses and Johannes.

VILLA TRAPP—The twenty-two-room mansion where the von Trapps lived in Aigen, Austria, sat empty for a while after the family escaped Austria in 1938. A year later a Catholic men's order, Missionaries of the Precious Blood, rented it from the von Trapps; however, they did not occupy it long before the Nazis forced them to leave. One of the most notorious Nazi leaders, Heinrich Himmler, took it over as his summer house. During the Nazi regime, he had the villa surrounded with barbed wire fences and armed guards, and a barracks was built in the back garden for the soldiers who lived there with Himmler.

In 1947, a couple of years after World War II ended, the Missionaries of the Precious Blood returned to the villa, this time purchasing it from the von Trapps, who had by now settled in Vermont. The order renovated the house in 1992 and then moved to another building while renting the villa to a business. In 2008 the villa was converted into a bed-and-breakfast and is now a popular tourist destination for von Trapp admirers and *Sound of Music* lovers everywhere.

TRAPP FAMILY MUSIC CAMP (1945–1956)—Not long after the von Trapps settled on their new farm, the Civilian Conservation Corps camp at which they had performed during their vacation in Stowe was abandoned. Hating to see it torn down, Maria had the idea of turning it into a music camp that would be similar to the "Sing Weeks" she had experienced as a young woman in Austria. Before long, the family had cleaned up the camp and had prepared it for their first summer season, which was devoted to music and folk dancing. The music camp soon became popular with American music lovers.

TRAPP FAMILY AUSTRIAN RELIEF (1946–1950)—In January 1947 the von Trapps received a letter from Major General Harry J. Collins, an American stationed in Austria, explaining how much the Austrians had suffered under Adolf Hitler's Nazi regime and were still suffering after its collapse. The general asked if the family might be able to raise some kind of assistance during their concert tours to send to Austria. Immediately, the family founded Trapp Family Austrian Relief, a nonprofit organization that had the stated purpose of "general help and relief to poor, displaced, and unfortunate people of all nationalities

and creeds in the United States and elsewhere".
This organization allowed the family to collect food,
clothing, and money from donors. During that season's concert tour, which was the longest one so
far, the von Trapps gave 107 performances and collected enormous amounts of donations to send to
Austria. They also donated the proceeds from their
souvenir sales. During the four years of its operation, the organization enabled the von Trapps to
send about 300,000 pounds of donations to help
their fellow Austrians.

TRAPP FAMILY LODGE (1950–present)—At first the von
Trapp's Vermont property was just a homestead
farm. The family made their living by continuing
their concert tours all over the world and by working their land between concert seasons. They tore
down the original farmhouse and built a Swiss chalet,
which they named *Cor Unum* (Latin for "one heart").
Gradually, Maria began inviting guests to the farm,
and soon it became so popular that the family had
to begin charging fees to cover their expenses. They
also had to establish an office and hire outside help.
In 1950 they named it the Trapp Family Lodge for
the public.

In 1980 tragedy struck when the Trapp Family
Lodge burned down in the coldest part of winter
with the rooms full of guests. In addition to one
fatality, the loss of the house was devastating, espe-

cially for Maria. By then Johannes was president of the lodge, and he decided to rebuild it larger and safer than the original building. He also decided to turn the entire property into more of a comfortable tourist destination. The Trapp Family Lodge property now has 2,600 acres and offers year-round recreation. The lodge includes an inn with ninety-six rooms, several time-share chalets, and a variety of trails for cross-country skiing, hiking, and running (with several annual races). The lodge also has a restaurant, a coffee shop, a gift shop, a brewery, and many other amenities. The current lodge opened in 1983 and remains a popular Vermont tourist destination for guests from all over the world.

THE SOUND OF MUSIC (musical, 1959; film, 1965)— With the publication of her autobiography *The Story of the Trapp Family Singers* in 1949, Maria was soon contacted by filmmakers in Hollywood who wanted to purchase the rights to make a movie about the family. She turned them down, but six years later a German film company bought the rights to the story, which was produced as a drama called *Die Trapp-Familie* with a sequel called *Die Trapp-Familie in Amerika*. These became two of the most popular movies ever produced in Germany, which increased Hollywood's interest. Over the next few years, Hollywood lost out to a theatrical version of the von Trapp story, which opened in 1959 as a Rogers and Hammerstein musical on Broadway called *The Sound of Music*. It starred Mary Martin as Maria. The musical was such a hit that it was produced as a movie by 20th Century Fox in 1965, starring Julie Andrews as Maria. The movie won five Oscars, including Best Picture, and it is one of the most beloved musicals of all time.

The von Trapps had mixed feelings about the musical, because the writers made major changes to the story and ended it with the family's escape from Austria. However, it rocketed them to even greater fame, making them a household name all over America and drawing many more people to their exquisite music, their inspiring story, and the beautiful Trapp Family Lodge.

ACKNOWLEDGMENTS

Though writing can feel like a solitary pursuit at times, every author needs help to bring a book to life. I am deeply grateful to those who helped me with this project: my mother, who passed on to me her love of children's literature and to whom I dedicate this book; my husband, Ethan, who has always supported my writing dreams; author Judith Robbins Rose and the South Metro Writer's Group of Littleton, Colorado, who taught me far more about writing than I realized; Kristina and Johannes von Trapp, who helped me get my facts straight; and Vivian Dudro, my editor, who gave me a chance.

BIBLIOGRAPHY

Gearin, Joan. "Movie vs. Reality: The Real Story of the von Trapp Family". *Prologue Magazine*, Winter 2005. National Archives, www.archives.gov/publications/prologue/2005/winter/von-trapps-html.

"The History of the Villa Trapp". Villa Trapp: The Original *Sound of Music* Family Home. villa-trapp.com/history/the-history-of-the-villa-trapp/?L=1.

Santopietro, Tom. *The "Sound of Music" Story*. New York: St. Martin's, 2015.

Trapp, Maria Augusta. *The Story of the Trapp Family Singers*. Philadelphia: J.B. Lippencott, 1949.

Trapp Family Lodge (website). Accessed January 2020. www.trappfamily.com.

von Trapp, Agathe. *Memories Before and After "The Sound of Music": An Autobiography*. Maryland: PublishAmerica, 2004.

von Trapp, Maria. *Maria: My Own Story*. Carol Stream, Ill.: Creation House, 1972.

vonTrapp.org. Georg and Agathe Foundation, 2015–2020. www.vontrapp.org/.